Play Jazz • Blues •

PIANO BY EAR

BOOK TWO

by ANDY OSTWALD

MW00445800

CD contents

Cover photo and design by the author
All music created and performed by the author

1 2 3 4 5 6 7 8 9 0

Visit us on the Web at www.melbay.com — E-mail us at email@melbay.com

PRAISE FOR PIANO BY EAR

Piano by Ear is a refreshingly innovative approach to jazz, blues, and rock piano. It effectively introduces improvising, ear training, and music theory, and features beautifully performed and recorded musical examples. I recommend *Piano by Ear* for self-study as well as for private and group instruction.

—Dee Spencer

Co-director, Jazz and World Music Studies program at S.F. State University
Executive Board Member, International Association of Jazz Educators

Piano by Ear is a welcome, modern, and original approach to ear training literature. It is a user-friendly, wisely written book series, and I highly recommend it.

—Mark Levine

author of "The Jazz Piano Book" and "The Jazz Theory Book"

Piano by Ear lays out clearly, for the first time in my memory, a method for developing the art of playing by ear as it relates to playing jazz, rock, and the blues. What's more, the recorded improvisations are of very high quality, both in technical realization and beauty—they are true piano playing and should prove both motivational and inspirational.

—Ken Durling

retailer of music method books and sheet music
composer

CONTENTS

ACKNOWLEDGEMENTS

Thanks to Bill Bay and the staff at Mel Bay Publications for their guidance from start to finish; to editors Wendy Weiner and John Raeside for their many contributions to the conversational tone and clarity of the text; to Jen Serota for the production work on the *Piano by Ear* cover design; to Shawn Hazen for his help with the layout of the books; and to John Ewing and David Bergen for answering all of my computer questions. I also want to thank Peck Allmond, Bill Freais, Ben Goldberg, Bridget Laky, Mark Levine, Robin Linnett, John McArdle, David Motto, Kenneth Nash, Steve Ostwald, Jenn Shreve, and Andrea Silvestri for their valuable contributions and insights.

Special thanks to Bud Spangler of *Syntropy Audio* for the loan of his great recording equipment and for his advice on microphone placement; to Dave Bell of *Bell Boy Recording* for mixing the CDs; and to Hans Christian of *Allemande Music* for mastering them.

Thanks also to the many students who have studied unpublished versions of *Piano by Ear* as their enthusiasm, questions, and musical development have been my guide and inspiration. Finally, thanks to my family and friends for their encouragement. *Piano by Ear* is dedicated to the memory of my dad, Kurt Ostwald.

ABOUT THE AUTHOR

Photo by Steve Ostwald

Jazz pianist, Andy Ostwald, performs in the San Francisco area and now-and-again on tour in the States and abroad. A teacher of jazz, blues, and rock piano for twenty years, he has also worked as an ensemble coach for the *Berkeley Jazz Workshop, Oaktown Jazz Workshops,* and the *Feather River Youth Jazz Camp,* and has conducted *Music for Dancers* workshops at the University of Santa Clara. Ostwald studied with jazz pianist Harold Mabern, classical pianist Sylvia Jenkins, and composer Lou Harrison. For more information about the author, please visit his website:

www.andyostwald.com

INTRODUCTION

Welcome to *Piano by Ear!* This comprehensive introduction to jazz, blues, and rock piano will offer easy-to-understand explanations of relevant music theory, and guide you step by step as you develop your skills. Above all, *Piano by Ear* will help you to explore and develop your ability to improvise. Rather than focus on written notation, you'll learn to express yourself at the piano by relying on your *ear* and on your own creative instincts.

BOOK TWO

Book Two of *Piano by Ear* is designed for students who have completed Book One or otherwise already have a basic foundation in improvising and learning by ear. (If you're new to *Piano by Ear,* a quick perusal of the Table of Contents and the first chapter will help you to determine whether Book Two is right for you.)

As for piano technique, you need just enough to play chords with your left hand and single notes with your right hand (nothing too fast). You'll also need a rudimentary knowledge of treble and bass clef so that you can read the written examples.

STUDYING BY EAR AND IMPROVISING GO HAND IN HAND

To gain the skill and understanding that lies at the heart of improvising, musicians study music by ear. This is how they learn to work with music based on how it sounds rather than how it looks on paper. It's also how they acquire a true feeling for the nuances and spirit of a given musical style.

There are numerous books on improvising that advocate learning by ear. The unique contribution of *Piano by Ear* is to show you how it's done. Complete with guidelines and recorded examples that demystify the practice, this book/CD series begins very simply, builds gradually, and ultimately helps prepare you for learning directly from the recordings of your favorite artists.

LEARN BY DOING

Along with learning by ear, improvising is something you learn by *doing. Piano by Ear* will serve as your guide as you progress from playing "two-chord jams" to full-blown jazz, rock, and blues improvisations. Each chapter will feature a new improvisation.

MUSIC THEORY

Music theory is only introduced as it becomes relevant to the music you're playing. This approach will guard against *information overload* and help you fully integrate what you're learning.

IMPROVISING TECHNIQUES

Like a good story, a compelling improvisation includes twists and turns, while maintaining a sense of continuity. *Piano by Ear* will show you a number of the techniques musicians use to create these improvisations, and guide you as you explore them in your own improvisations.

COMPOSING

Piano by Ear will encourage you to do a little composing. Specifically, it will suggest that you make up and write down melodic phrases that you can then weave into your improvisations. This practice is invaluable—it gives you a way to develop musical ideas apart from the moment-to-moment concerns of improvising. (Previous experience with composing is not necessary.)

THE ACCOMPANYING CD

The improvisations recorded on the accompanying CD are intended to be a source of inspiration as well as a means of instruction. They were created with the idea that uncomplicated music—even music that is simple enough to introduce the practice of learning by ear—can spark the imagination and be a joy to listen to.

A PROVEN METHOD

I have used *Piano by Ear* with my students for years with exciting results. The youngest student was twelve, the oldest, about sixty. Some studied with the ambition of developing a professional career. Others played solely for their own enjoyment. Hearing the feedback and watching the creative development of these students served as my guide and inspiration in revising, expanding, and fine-tuning the series for this publication.

EQUIPMENT

- a piano or keyboard
- a CD player that can be set up at your piano (a portable player is fine)
- a pair of headphones

Chapter One

Major Triads & Major-Seven Chords

We are all improvisers. The most common form of improvisation is ordinary speech. As we talk and listen, we are drawing on a set of building blocks (vocabulary) and rules for combining them (grammar). These have been given to us by our culture. But the sentences we make with them may never have been said before and may never be said again. Every conversation is a form of jazz. The activity of instantaneous creation is as ordinary to use as breathing.

—Stephen Nachmanovitch
from "Free Play"

NEW POSSIBILITIES

In *Piano by Ear's* Book One, music was created entirely from the key's corresponding major scale. For example, the improvisations and chords in the key of C major were created entirely from the notes of the C major scale. The chords that were featured are reviewed below:

Triads

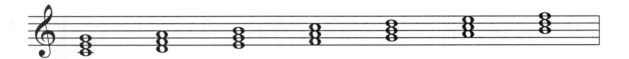

Seventh Chords

In Book Two, a key's corresponding scale will provide a bases for the music we create, however, notes from outside the scale will also be used. This means that notes such as D♭, F♯ and B♭ may be used in an improvisation that is in the key of C major. This will open up a new world of musical possibilities. It will also necessitate some changes in how we think about, and how we structure, the music that we're creating.

BUILDING CHORDS

For starters, rather than build chords from the key's corresponding scale as in Book One, each chord will be built from its own scale: D♭ chords will be built from D♭ scales, G chords will be built from G scales, and so on, *regardless of what key the chords are used in.*

In a moment, you'll be asked to build chords from all twelve major scales. Keep in mind that all major scales conform to the same sequence of half steps and whole steps—specifically, scale tones *3* and *4,* and *7* and *1* are a half step apart, and the other scale tones are a whole step apart. The C major scale is used in the following illustration (h = half step; W = whole step):

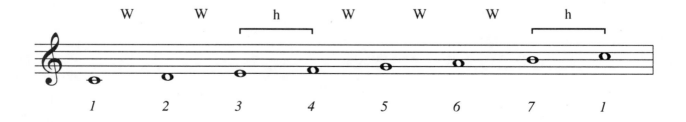

MAJOR TRIADS & MAJOR-SEVEN CHORDS

Chapter One will feature *major triads* and *major-seven chords.* To build a major triad, stack *1, 3,* and *5* of the major scale—these notes become the *root, 3rd,* and *5th* of the chord. Likewise, to build a major-seven chord, stack the *1, 3, 5,* and *7* of the major scale—these notes become the *root, 3rd, 5th,* and *7th* of the chord.

The twelve major scales and their corresponding major triads and major-seven chords are built below. Notice that major triads are written without an accompanying symbol, and major-seven chords are identified by adding " Δ7 ." [1] (These chords are not associated with any particular key right now—we'll use them in a key later in the chapter.)

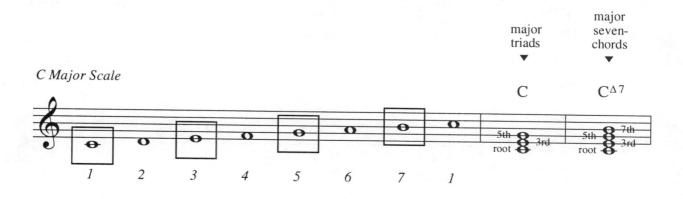

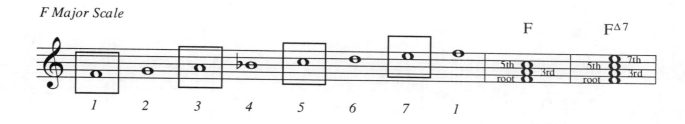

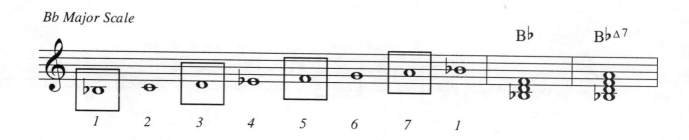

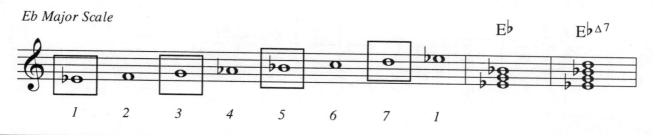

---

[1] Major-seven chords are also identified as follows: maj7, MA7.

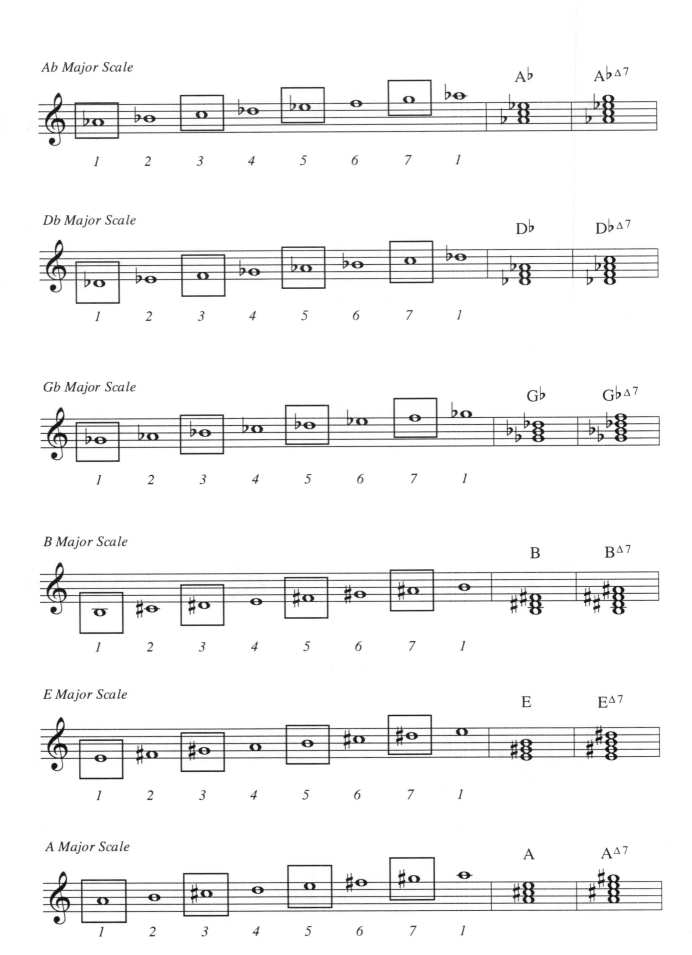

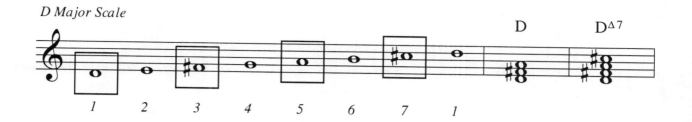

D Major Scale

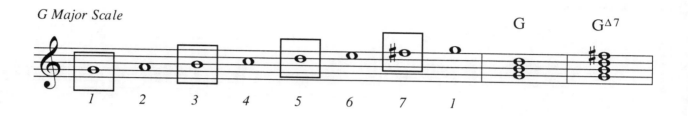

G Major Scale

THE CYCLE OF FIFTHS

The twelve major triads and major-seven chords were just introduced in the following sequence:

C   F   B♭   E♭   A♭   D♭   G♭   B   E   A   D   G   (C)

This sequence of notes is called the *Cycle of Fifths,* or *the Cycle* for short. Since composers often base parts of their chord accompaniments on the Cycle, it is useful to practice chords in this order.

Take a few minutes to memorize the sequence of notes in the Cycle of Fifths. This is relatively easy to do if you group the notes into pairs and then keep in mind that these pairs descend by whole steps, as illustrated and explained below:

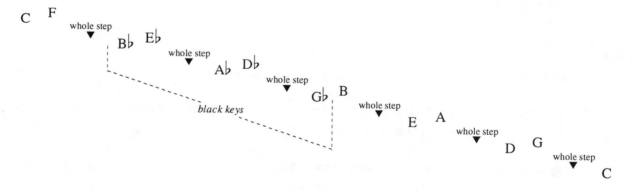

Play the first pair of notes in the Cycle. Specifically, play C then move up to the nearest F. Now play the note that is a whole step below C, i.e., B♭, then the note that is a whole step below F, i.e., E♭. As you can see in the above illustration, B♭ and E♭ are the second pair of notes in the Cycle. Continue descending by whole steps until you return to C (an octave lower).

As you memorize the Cycle, keep in mind that the five black keys appear consecutively, and that only the fourth pair of notes in the Cycle (G♭ and B) contain both a black key and a white key.[1]

---

[1] The first six chords of Book One's chord study called *Song Pattern Chords* were based on the Cycle of Fifths.

CHORD STUDIES

Learn to play the twelve major triads and major-seven chords (Δ7) from memory *through the Cycle.* The chord studies are written below and demonstrated on Track 1 of the accompanying CD. Set up your CD player so that you can use it while sitting at your piano; then listen to Track 1 as you read along below:

Major Triads

Major-Seven Chords

When you practice the major triads and major-seven chords:

- Say the letter name of each chord just before you play it (as demonstrated on Track 1). Listen closely to the sound of the chords as you play them.

- Be aware of the names of the chord tones you are playing: major triads feature the *root, 3rd,* and *5th;* major-seven chords (Δ7) feature the *root, 3rd, 5th* and *7th.*

- Practice your hands separately, then together.

- Choose a tempo that enables you to play without mistakes or hesitations. If a given tempo is too challenging, slow down—it's more important to play fluently than to play quickly. Only increase the tempo as your ability allows.

- Learn to play the studies from memory.

CHORD VOICINGS

Recall from Book One that each arrangement of the notes of a chord gives you a different *chord voicing*. Triads generate three voicings: root position, first inversion, and second inversion. The names are shortened here to "root," "first," and "second":

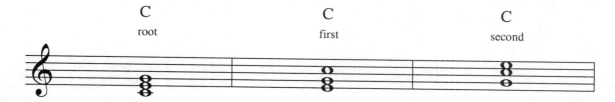

Seventh chords generate four voicings: root position, first inversion, second inversion, and third inversion:

ROMAN NUMERALS

Recall from Book One that chords are identified with Roman numerals to indicate their position within a key. The numerals are generated from the key's corresponding scale. In the key of C major, for example, a chord built on the first note of the C major scale is a "**I**" chord; a chord built on the second note of the C major scale is a "**II**" chord, and so on:

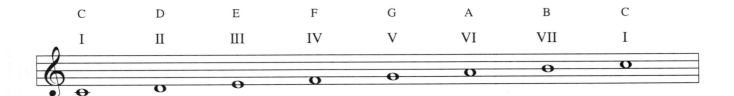

As mentioned earlier in this chapter, the music in Book Two will include notes that are outside the key's corresponding scale. These "outsiders" may even be used as the roots of chords. For example, an improvisation in the key of C may include a chord that is built on D♭. This chord would be identified as the ♭**II**. Similarly, a chord built on E♭ would be identified as the ♭**III**, and so on:[1]

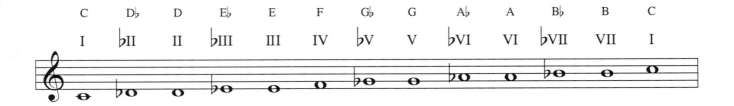

Notice that flat signs (♭) appear *after* letter names, and *before* Roman numeral names. The chords are spoken as they're written, so for example, D♭ is pronounced "D-flat," while ♭**II** is pronounced "flat-two."

---

[1] The ♭**II** is sometimes called the ♯**I**, the ♭**III** is sometimes called the ♯**II**, and so on.

LEARNING ACCOMPANIMENTS BY EAR

Like Book One, Book Two will encourage you to learn the featured chord accompaniments by ear. Step-by-step guidelines and a special recording of the accompaniment will help you with this valuable ear training. Listen to the recording through headphones—they'll make identifying chords much easier!

This chapter's accompaniment is in the key of C major, and the chords are major triads and major-seven chords (Δ7). The accompaniment is recorded on Track 2—you'll hear the root of each chord just before the chord itself.

Step 1   **Identify the Root**

 Play Track 2 and rest your finger on the CD player's pause button. Listen to the root of the first chord—it's the low note at the beginning of the track. Press *pause* before the chord itself is played.

With the sound of the root resonating in your ear, find it on the piano. Keep in mind that the note in question isn't necessarily a member of the C major scale—it can be any note. Also, know that it's located in the second octave below middle C.

Don't worry if you can't identify the root right away—keep listening. Read on when you think you've identified the root.

_____

If you said that the root is C, you're right. C is the root of the **I** chord, so "I" is written above the first measure:

I

A ___ ___ ___   B ___ ___ ___ ___ ___

𝄢   𝄢

 Use the above approach to determine the other Roman numeral names in the accompaniment. (You'll hear a momentary pause between Sections A and B on the recording.) Write your answers above the lines provided. Check your work on the next page.

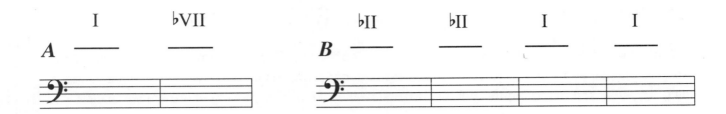

Step 2   Identify the Top Note

Play Track 2 and listen to the first chord. Press *pause* before the root of the second chord is played. The note you are hearing most prominently is the top note. With the sound of this note resonating in your ear, find it on the piano—it's located in the general vicinity of middle C. Find the note before you read on.

If you said that the top note is G, you're right. G is placed in the first measure:

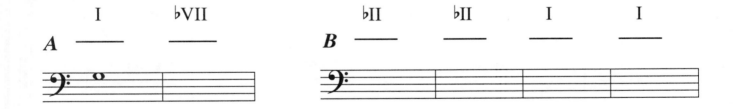

Use the above approach to determine the top notes of the other chords in the accompaniment. Fill in your answers above. Check your work on the next page.

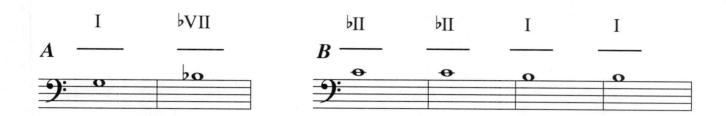

Step 3   Build the Chords from the Top Down / Determine the Chords by Ear

You now know that the first chord is a **I** chord, and that its top note is G. You also know from an earlier discussion that the chords in this accompaniment are major triads and major-seven chords (∆7). This tells you that the first chord must be one of the following:

Play these chords on the piano and listen closely—notice that the major-seven chord has a denser, more complex sound than the triad.

 Now play Track 2 and listen to the first chord. Press *pause* before the root of the second chord is played. With the sound of the first chord resonating in your ear, play the two possible chords on the piano again. Let your ear determine which of the two chords matches the chord on the recording. This can be challenging, so be patient. Keep listening until you think you know the identity of the first chord; then check your work below.

――――――――――

The first chord of the accompaniment is the **I** major triad in root position; consequently, "root" is written underneath the **I**, and the remaining notes of the chord are added to the staff underneath the top note, G:

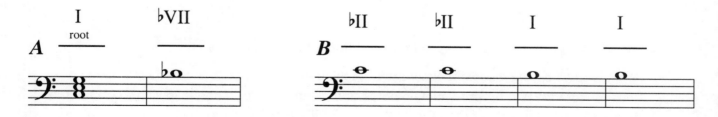

 Repeat Step 3 for each chord in the accompaniment, and complete the chords above.[1] Remember to add "∆7" next to the Roman numeral of any major-seven chord. Check your work on the next page.

――――――――――

[1] In some instances, identifying the top note will tell you the chord's identity. The ♭II chord in this accompaniment serves as an example: you know that the top note is C, and you also know that C is in the ♭II∆7 chord, but not in the ♭II triad, which means that the chord in question must be the ♭II∆7 chord.

The "%" symbol in Section B means *repeat the previous measure:*

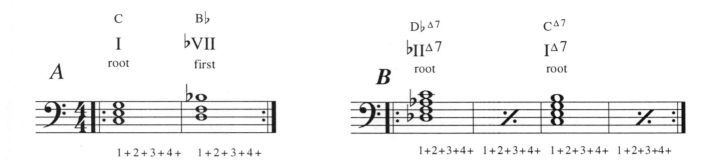

Learn to play the accompaniment fluently from memory. Chose a relaxed tempo and count to yourself: "1 and 2 and 3 and 4 and." Play the chords softly so that they'll effectively recede into the background when you improvise.

THE SUSTAIN PEDAL

The Basic Pattern

Students who are not versed in the art of pedaling are encouraged to use the following basic pedaling pattern to create a smooth transition from one chord to the next: Engage the pedal just before you let go of a chord, and release it when you play the next chord. This will connect one chord to the next without blurring together too many of the notes you're playing with your right hand. Pedaling is indicated with a bracket below the stave—the pedal is engaged where the bracket begins and released where the bracket ends:

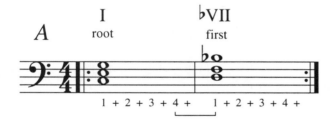

When Filling out the Accompaniment (see bottom of page 22)

When you *fill out the accompaniment,* try breaking away from the basic pedaling pattern (described above) in order to sustain notes of the same chord. In the following example, the pedal sustains the notes of the **I** triad throughout the first measure. Since all of the notes belong to the same chord, pedaling them together will not compromise the clarity of the chord.

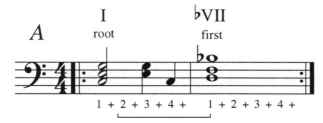

NOTES FOR IMPROVISING

Improvising in Book One involved using the notes of the key's corresponding major scale. In the key of C major, for example, you simply drew from the notes of the C major scale throughout the improvisation.

In this chapter's C major improvisation, you will be using a separate scale with each chord. The illustration below shows the featured accompaniment, which you learned on the previous page. The letters stacked above the chords are the scales that are suggested for improvising.

Read the stack of notes above the **I** (C) triad. Read from bottom to top and notice that the stack is simply the seven notes of the C major scale: C, D, E, F, G, A, and B. Consequently, when you improvise over the **I** triad, draw from the notes of the C major scale. This scale is also used for improvising over the **I**Δ7 chord. *Though the illustration shows one octave, you're free to play the notes in any octave.*

The scale stacked above the ♭**VII** (B♭) triad can be thought of as an altered C major scale—one in which B has been lowered to B♭. Use the notes of this scale when you improvise over the ♭**VII** triad. *Tip: When your left hand alternates between the **I** triad to the ♭**VII** triad in Section A, you can focus on alternating between the note B and the note B♭ in your right hand. The other six notes in Section A's two improvisation scales are the same.*

The scale suggested for improvising over the ♭**II**Δ7 (D♭Δ7) chord has the same seven notes as the A♭ major scale. *Tip: When your left hand alternates between the ♭**II**Δ7 chord and the **I**Δ7 chord in Section B, you can think in terms of alternating between the notes of the A♭ major scale and the notes of the C major scale in your right hand. It is also helpful to keep in mind that the notes C, F, and G are common to both of Section B's improvisation scales.*

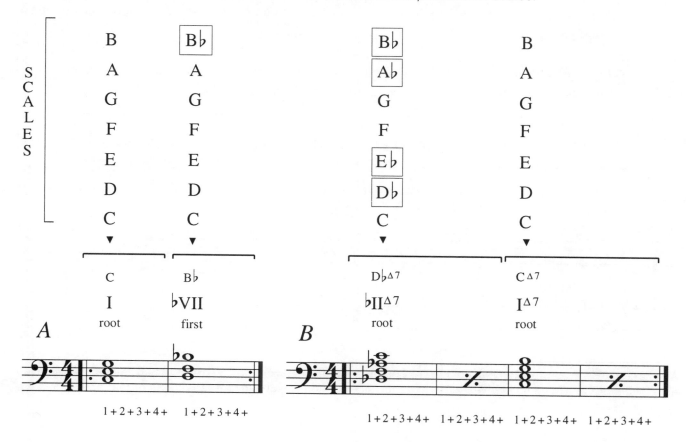

As you can see in the previous illustration, notes that are outside the key's corresponding scale appear in a box, making them easy to spot. Since this improvisation is in the key of C major, the notes in a box are those outside the C major scale.

When you improvise, stay in each section for as long as you like. You may want to repeat Section A two or three times before moving on to Section B. Then again, you may want to repeat Section A a dozen times before you move on. Do whatever sounds good in the moment. Go back and forth between sections as many times as you like: A - B - A - B, and so on. End your improvisation on the I triad if you end in Section A; end on the IΔ7 chord if you end in Section B.

Finally, if you play a note that you like that has not been suggested by *Piano by Ear,* feel free to use it! The suggested notes are not intended to dictate which notes you ultimately can and cannot play, but rather to provide guidance as you develop your improvising skills.

MORE ABOUT THE FEATURED IMPROVISATION SCALES

Each scale used for improvising includes the notes of its underlying chord, plus notes that are complementary to that chord. For example, the notes suggested for improvising over the ♭IIΔ7 (D♭Δ7) chord include the four notes in that chord (D♭, F, A♭, and C) plus three notes that are complementary to the chord.

The scale used for improvising over a chord isn't necessarily the scale used to build that chord. For example, we used the D♭ major scale to build the ♭IIΔ7 (D♭Δ7) chord (see page 10), yet we used a scale equivalent to the A♭ major scale to improvise over the chord. Choosing a scale for improvising over a particular chord is based on the type of chord (major, minor etc.), the harmonic context in which the chord is used, the style of music, and personal taste.

If you're familiar with scale theory and its terminology, and are curious about the names of the scales used in each of Book Two's improvisations, refer to the appendix on page 107.

The following example was created by using notes from the improvising scales suggested on the previous page. Notice that this example features a transition from Section A to Section B:[1]

---

[1] Any flat, sharp, or natural sign placed in front of a note (as distinct from being part of the key signature) is called an *accidental.* An accidental applies to the note it precedes and all subsequent repetitions of that note within the same measure.

IMPROVISATION WORKSHOP:

The improvisation techniques introduced in Book One and reviewed below will help you create improvisations with both variety and a sense of continuity. The musical examples used to illustrate the techniques are in the key of C major and feature the chords from Section A of this chapter's accompaniment.

VARYING THE LENGTH OF YOUR PHRASES AND SPACES

This creates variety and contributes to a sense of rhythmic freedom.

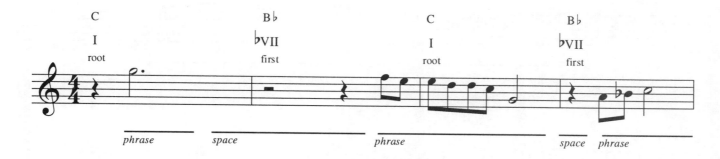

BEGINNING PHRASES ON DIFFERENT BEATS OF THE MEASURE

Like the previous technique, this one creates variety and contributes to a sense of rhythmic freedom.

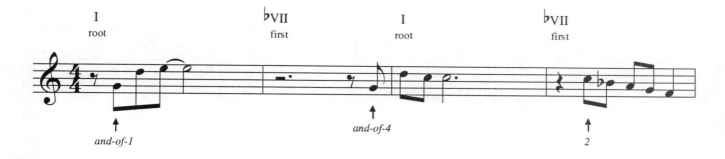

REPEATING PHRASES AND PARTS OF PHRASES

Repetition creates continuity. In the following example, the phrases begin the same and end differently.

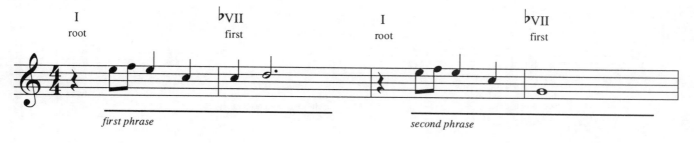

REPEATING MELODIC CONTOURS AND/OR RHYTHMIC PATTERNS

Like the previous technique, this one involves creating continuity through the use of repetition. Your repeated melodic contours and/or repeated rhythmic patterns needn't be identical—just similar. In the following example, the two phrases have similar rhythms (though they begin on different beats of their respective measures) and similar contours. Draw a line from one note to the next within each phrase and you will see that both phrases have the following general contour:

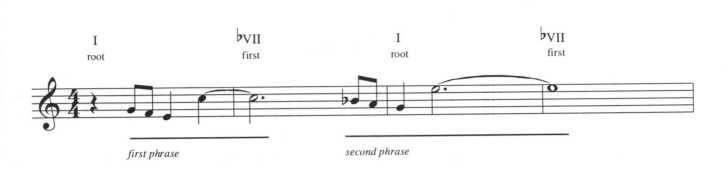

INCLUDING EIGHTH-NOTE SYNCOPATION

Eighth-note syncopation is the rhythmic effect created by drawing attention to an off-beat. This is done by playing a note on an off-beat, and *not* playing on one or both of the surrounding beats. Eighth-note syncopation is native to jazz, rock, and the blues—it contributes to the spontaneity and rhythmic drive of the music. Examples of eighth-note syncopation are marked below with asterisks (*):

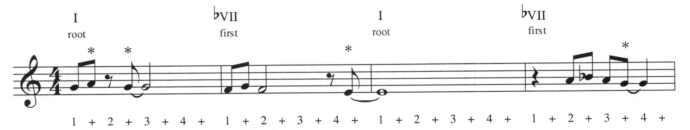

FILLING OUT THE ACCOMPANIMENT

Filling out the accompaniment refers to repeating a chord—or some part of a chord—after it has been played on the first beat of the measure. Leave some measures *unfilled*—they'll provide a welcome contrast to the measures you *do* fill.

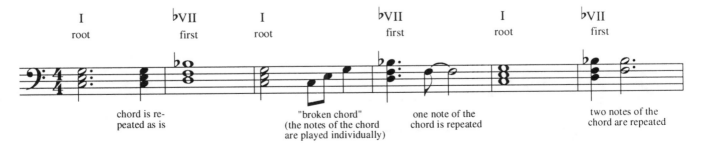

Book Two will introduce a few additional improvising techniques. The first one is...

IMPROVISATION WORKSHOP:

INCLUDING PHRASES THAT FLOW FROM ONE SCALE INTO THE NEXT

Now that you'll be switching from one scale to another when you improvise, make a point of creating phrases that begin with notes from one scale and continue with notes from the following scale. Doing so will open the door to a number of interesting melodic possibilities.

 Track 3 is an improvisation that uses the same accompaniment and scales you're using for your improvisations in this chapter. (The featured scales are illustrated on page 19.) Listen to Track 3 —listen in particular for phrases that flow from one scale directly into the next. The following four-measure phrase serves as an example. You'll hear it at the very end of the improvisation:

LISTENING

Listen frequently to the improvisation on Track 3 for ideas and inspiration. Keep in mind that it uses the same accompaniment and guidelines you're using for your improvisations.

 Also listen frequently to the improvisation on Track 4—it is *based* on the accompaniment and guidelines you're using, but isn't *limited* to them. You don't need to understand how this improvisation was created, or play anything that sounds remotely like it—just listen, and know that it's directly related to the improvisation on Track 3, and to the improvisations you're creating. *Listen to Track 4 at this time.*

Finally, listen frequently to your favorite artists—both on recordings, and if possible, in concert. Become intimately familiar with the music that inspires you. Also, challenge your ears with music that's unfamiliar. Ask those whose opinion you respect for their recommendations regarding worthwhile recordings and upcoming performances.

Listening to music plays a key role in learning to improvise. Although you'll benefit the most when you set aside all distractions and immerse yourself in the music, even the most casual listening will promote an intuitive musical understanding that's invaluable.

> The improvisations on Tracks 3 and 4 are offered to inform and inspire, *not* set a standard of musicianship that you're expected to meet. Leave expectations behind! Aim to be both *alert* and completely *relaxed* when you improvise. Immerse yourself in the sounds you are creating, and keep in mind that everything you play provides valuable experience.

THE PRACTICING PAGE

Practicing frequently will help you maintain a sense of continuity from one practice session to the next. Keep in mind that even a ten-minute practice session can be productive—particularly when you focus on one or two activities. When time allows, practice all of the chapter's activities.[1] They're reviewed below:

CHORD STUDIES

Learn to play major triads and major-seven chords through the Cycle (p. 12).

LISTENING

Listen to the improvisations on Tracks 3 and 4 for ideas and inspiration, and to gain an intuitive feel for the music. Remember that Track 3 was created out of the same set of guidelines you're using for your improvisations, and Track 4 is based on, but not limited to, these guidelines.

IMPROVISING

Play this chapter's accompaniment and count silently (p. 18). Join in with your right hand and improvise, using the suggested scales (p. 19); remember to end the improvisation on the **I** triad if you end in Section A, and on the **I**D7 chord if you end in Section B. Let your ear be your guide as you improvise. Also, make use of the improvising techniques that are offered on pages 21-23 and listed here:

New! • Include phrases that flow directly from one scale into the next

- Fill out the accompaniment

- Repeat melodic contours and rhythmic patterns

- Repeat phrases and parts of phrases

- Include eighth-note syncopation

- Begin phrases on different beats of the measure

- Vary the length of your phrases and spaces

As in Book One, it isn't necessary to consider all techniques at once as you improvise. Shift your focus from one to another, or if you prefer, create short improvisations and explore a different technique in each one.

Play from Memory!

For best results, devote a part of each practice session to memorizing the guidelines to the activities listed above. You'll want to eventually turn to this page and practice the activities from memory. Learning the guidelines in this way will promote a solid grasp of the material, and playing from memory will strengthen your ear.

Move on to Chapter Two when you've explored the featured improvisation to your own satisfaction, and when you're able to play the chord studies with confidence. This may take a few days, a week, or more to accomplish. Spend as much time as you need!

---

[1] Book One suggested transcribing your own phrases and phrases from the recorded improvisations. We'll return to this practice in Chapter Three.

Chapter Two

Dominant-Seven Chords

Buddy [Guy] is able to summon up, apparently at will, an intensity of emotion that would be the envy of any great artist. The length of time he can pause, the way he'll lay a silence against a flurry of notes, the way a note that apparently is randomly chosen from a run suddenly becomes important as though the thought or feeling has just leaped into his hands.... Those are great moments of Buddy Guy and great moments of blues in general.

—Bruce Iglauer
founder of Alligator Records

CHORD STUDIES

DOMINANT-SEVEN CHORDS

The symbol for the dominant-seven chord is " 7 ." To build this chord, begin with the major-seven chord (Δ7); then lower the 7th a half step. The lowered 7th is identified as the "♭7th":

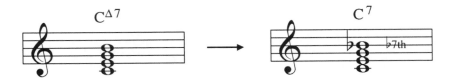

Build all twelve dominant-seven chords and check your work below. (The D♭7 chord includes a C♭, which is the same note as B, and the G♭7 chord includes an F♭, which is the same note as E.)

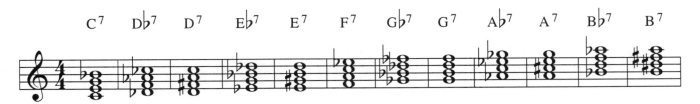

Learn to play the dominant-seven chords through the Cycle. Build the left hand's C7 on middle C, and the right hand's C7 an octave higher. From these starting positions, move *up* to F7, *down* to B♭7, *up* to E♭7, *down* to A♭7, and so on, until you arrive back at C7 an octave lower (as you did with the major-seven chords in Chapter One):

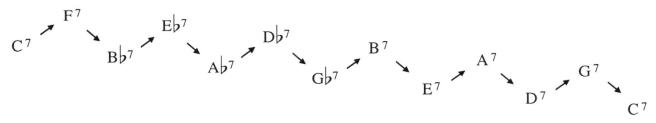

Reminders:

- Say the letter name of each chord before you play it—listen closely to the sound of the chord.
- Be aware of the names of the chord tones you are playing: dominant-seven chords (7) feature the *root, 3rd, 5th* and *♭7th.*
- Practice your hands separately, then together.
- Choose a tempo that enables you to play in a relaxed and fluent manner.
- Learn to play the chord study from memory.

REVIEW

Review major triads and major-seven chords (Δ7) by playing them from memory through the Cycle.

THE ACCOMPANIMENT

This chapter's chord accompaniment is in the key of F major, which means that a chord built on F is a **I** chord, a chord built on G♭ is a ♭**II** chord, and so on:[1]

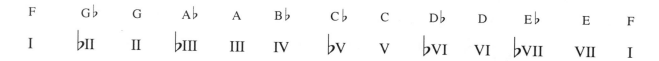

F	G♭	G	A♭	A	B♭	C♭	C	D♭	D	E♭	E	F
I	♭II	II	♭III	III	IV	♭V	V	♭VI	VI	♭VII	VII	I

The accompaniment may include any major triad, major-seven chord (Δ7), or dominant-seven chord (7). Track 5 and the following guidelines will help you learn the accompaniment by ear. The low notes played in front of the chords are the roots of the chords. As always when you transcribe, listen to the recording through headphones.

Step 1   **Identify the Root**

Slip on your headphones and play Track 5, resting a finger on the CD player's pause button. Listen to the root of the first chord (the low note at the beginning of the track), then press *pause* before the first chord is played.

With the sound of the root resonating in your ear, find it on the piano. Remember that the note in question can be any note—it isn't necessarily a member of the F major scale. Also, know that the note is located in the second octave below middle C.

Read on when you think that you've identified the root.

You're right if you said that the root is F. F is the root of the **I** chord, so "I" is written above the first measure:

Use the above approach to determine the Roman numerals in the remaining measures. Write your answers above the lines provided. Check your work on the next page.

---

[1] Recall from Book One that the key signature of a major key is determined by the sharps or flats in the key's corresponding major scale. Since there's a B♭ in the F major scale, there's also a B♭ in the key signature of the key of F major. The F major key signature will be used throughout Chapter Two.

Step 2 Identify the Top Note

Play Track 5 and listen to the first chord. Press *pause* before the root of the second chord is played. The note you are hearing most prominently is the top note. With the sound of this note resonating in your ear, find it on the piano—it's located in the general vicinity of middle C. Find the note before you read on.

_____

If you said that the top note is C, you're right. C is placed in the first measure:

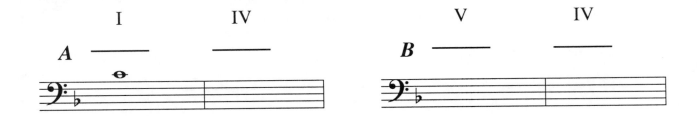

Use the above approach to determine the top notes of the other chords in the accompaniment. (Remember that B♭ is in the key signature.) Fill in your answers above. Check your work on the next page.

Step 3 **Build the Chords from the Top Down / Determine the Chords by Ear**

You now know that the first chord is a **I** chord, and that its top note is C. You also know that the chords in this accompaniment can be major triads, major-seven chords (Δ7), or dominant-seven chords (7). This tells you that the first chord is one of the following:

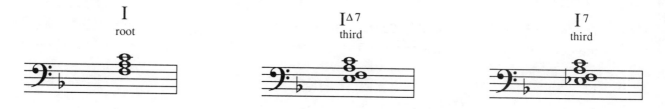

Play these chords on the piano and listen closely to how they differ in sound.

 Now listen to the first chord on Track 5—press *pause* before the root of the second chord is played. With the sound of this chord resonating in your ear, play the three possible chords on the piano again. Let your ear determine which of these chords matches the first chord on the recording. Keep listening and playing until you think you know the identity of the first chord. Check your work below.

The first chord is the **I7** in third inversion. Consequently, "7" is added to the **I**; "third" is written underneath the **I**; and the remaining notes of the chord are added to the stave underneath the top note, C:

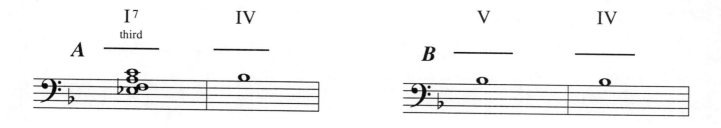

 Repeat Step 3 for each chord in the accompaniment, and write your results in the measures above. Check your work on the next page.

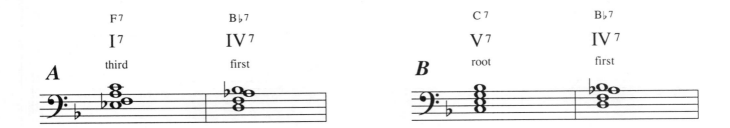

12/8 TIME

The improvisations in *Piano by Ear* have featured 4/4 time and 3/4 time. In both of these meters, the count is equal to a quarter note. The quarter note, in turn, subdivides into two eighth notes:

This chapter's improvisation will feature *12/8 time.* Here, the count equals a dotted quarter note, which subdivides into three eighth notes. 12/8 is counted: "1-and-a-2-and-a-3-and-a-4-and-a," and is written:

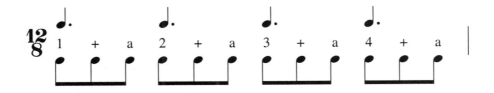

THE ACCOMPANIMENT

Learn to play the accompaniment fluently from memory. Choose a relaxed tempo and count silently in 12/8 time. Play the chords softly so that they'll effectively recede into the background when you improvise. Use the sustain pedal to create a smooth transition from one chord to the next.

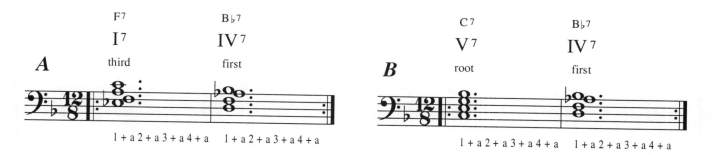

When you use the accompaniment for your improvisations, stay in each section for as long as you like. Also, go back and forth between sections as many times as you like: A - B - A - B, and so on. End your improvisation on the **I**7 chord in Section A.

THE BLUES SCALE

This chapter's improvisation is an introduction to playing the blues. Along with the particular chord accompaniments that are associated with the blues, the *blues scale* lies at the heart of the music.[1]

The blues scale may seem a little odd at first. It doesn't have a *2* or a *6,* and yet includes both a *5* and a *b5.* Here's the C blues scale:

This chapter's improvisation is in the key of F and consequently will feature the F blues scale (remember the Bb in the key signature):

---

[1] There's a brief introduction to blues accompaniments in Chapter Eight. Book Three will cover the subject in greater detail.

PLAY WITH THESE RHYTHMS

This workshop features two rhythms that are key to playing in 12/8 time. The last note in each rhythm is played on the "a" of a beat, and held into the following beat. This creates a syncopated feel that's native to jazz, rock, and the blues. You can play the rhythms on any beat of the measure—that's why "x" is used instead of a specific count in the following illustration:

TRACK 6

The rhythms just introduced are bracketed in the following example. Notice that they occur on different beats of the measure.

 The above example is a transcription of the first few measures of the improvisation recorded on Track 6. Listen to the track and keep your ears peeled for the two rhythms introduced above. Also, notice the relaxed *laid-back feel* of the improvisation.

THE PRACTICING PAGE

For best results, devote a part of each practice session to memorizing the guidelines to the activities listed below. You'll want to eventually turn to this page and practice the activities from memory. Learning the guidelines in this way will promote a solid grasp of the material, and playing *by heart* will strengthen your ear.

CHORD STUDIES

Learn to play dominant-seven chords through the Cycle (p. 26).

Review major triads and major-seven chords (p. 26).

LISTENING

Listen to the improvisations on Tracks 6 and 7 for ideas and inspiration, and to gain an intuitive feel for the music. Track 6 was created from the same set of guidelines you're using for your improvisations. Track 7 is based on, but not limited to, these guidelines.

IMPROVISING

Play this chapter's accompaniment and count silently (p. 31). Join in with your right

hand and improvise, using the notes of the F blues scale (page 31). Let your ear be your guide as you improvise. Also, make use of the following techniques:

New! • Play with the two rhythms featured on page 32

• Fill out the accompaniment

• Repeat melodic contours and rhythmic patterns

• Repeat phrases and parts of phrases

• Include eighth-note syncopation

• Begin phrases on different beats of the measure

• Vary the length of your phrases and spaces

Move on to Chapter Three when you've explored the featured improvisation to your own satisfaction, and when you're able to play the chord studies with confidence.

Chapter Three

Minor Triads & Minor-Seven Chords

I used to listen to those Charlie Parker, Bud Powell, and Dexter Gordon records on *Savoy* and pick out the chords note for note. My teachers were all those great guys on records.

—Horace Silver
pianist

CHORD STUDIES

MINOR TRIADS

The symbol for the minor triad is " - ." [1] To build this chord, begin with the major triad; then lower the 3rd a half step:

Build all twelve minor triads and learn to play them fluently through the Cycle. Remember that the left hand begins the Cycle on middle C; the right hand begins an octave higher:

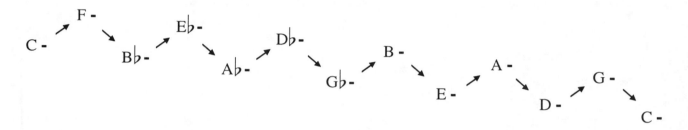

MINOR-SEVEN CHORDS

The symbol for the minor-seven chord is " -7 ." [2] To build this chord, begin with the dominant-seven chord (7); then lower the 3rd a half step:

Build all twelve minor-seven chords and learn to play them fluently through the Cycle:

---

[1] Minor triads are also identified as follows: m, min, MI
[2] Minor-seven chords are also identified as follows: m7, min7, MI7

Chord Study Reminders:

- Say the letter name of each chord before you play it—listen closely to the sound of the chord.

- Be aware of the names of the chord tones you are playing: minor triads (-) feature the *root*, ♭*3rd*, and *5th*; minor-seven chords (-7) feature the *root*, ♭*3rd*, *5th* and ♭*7th*.

- Practice your hands separately, then together.

- Choose a tempo that enables you to play in a relaxed and fluent manner.

- Learn to play the studies from memory.

REVIEW

Review the chords introduced in previous chapters by playing them from memory through the Cycle. You may want to review just one type of chord in each practice session:

- dominant-seven chords (7)
- major-seven chords (Δ7)
- major triads

THE ACCOMPANIMENT

 This chapter's chord accompaniment is in the key of G major. Learn the accompaniment from Track 8 and transcribe it below. (The first chord in Section B has been transcribed to serve as an example.) The transcribing guidelines are summarized on the following page. You can also look back to pages 27-31 for guidance.

Section A may include any seventh chord introduced so far in Book Two:

- major-seven chords (Δ7)
- dominant-seven chords (7)
- minor-seven chords (-7)

Section B may include any triad introduced so far in Book Two:

- major triads
- minor triads (-)

Remember that F♯ is in the key signature.

Step 1   **Identify the Root**

Listen to the root of the first chord, and press *pause* before the chord itself is played. Find the note on the piano—it's located in the second octave below middle C. Once you've identified the root, write the corresponding Roman numeral above the first measure—leave room beneath the Roman numeral so that you'll have room to write in the voicing (root, first, etc.) when the time comes. Repeat Step 1 for the other chords in the accompaniment.

Step 2   **Identify the Top Note**

Listen to the first chord; the note you are hearing most prominently is the top note. With the sound of this note resonating in your ear, find it on the piano—it's located in the general vicinity of middle C. Once you've determined the top note, write it in the first measure. Repeat Step 2 to identify the top notes of the other chords in the accompaniment.

Step 3   **Build the Chords from the Top Down / Determine the Chords by Ear**

You now know the Roman numeral and top note of the first chord. You also know—thanks to the information near the beginning of *The Accompaniment* section—which type of chord the first chord may be. Build each of these possible chords from the top note down; then play the chords on the piano and listen closely to how they differ in sound.

Now listen to the first chord on the recording. With the sound of this chord resonating in your ear, play the possible chords on the piano again. Let your ear determine which of these chords matches the first chord on the recording. Keep listening and playing until you think you know the identity of the first chord.

Now add the appropriate symbol (Δ7, 7, etc.) after the first chord's Roman numeral; the appropriate voicing (root, first, etc.) underneath the Roman numeral; and the remaining notes of the chord underneath the top note. Write lightly in pencil and keep an eraser handy. Repeat Step 3 for each chord in the accompaniment. Check your work on the following page.

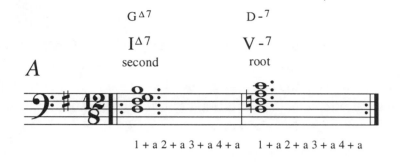

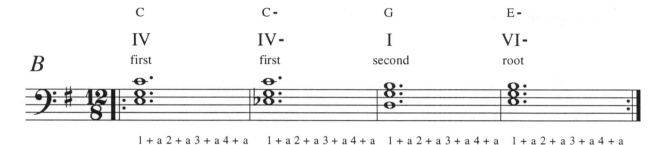

Learn to play the accompaniment fluently from memory. Chose a relaxed tempo and count to yourself in 12/8 time. Play the chords softly, and use the sustain pedal to create a smooth transition from one chord to the next.

NOTES FOR IMPROVISING

The following guidelines refer to the illustration on the next page. As in Chapter One, the columns of notes above the accompaniment are the scales suggested for improvising. Each scale includes the notes of the underlying chord, plus notes that are complementary in the context of this improvisation. (Though the illustration shows one octave, you're free to play the notes in any octave.)

The improvisation is in the key of G major, and as you can see on the next page, the G major scale is suggested for improvising over the I∆7 (G∆7), IV (C), I (G), and VI- (E-) chords.

The scale suggested for the V-7 (D-7) chord has the same seven notes as the C major scale. You can think of it either as the C major scale or as a modified G major scale—one in which F♯ has been lowered to F.

The scale suggested for the IV- (C-) triad is unlike any major scale. Think of it as a modified G major scale—one in which F♯ has been lowered to F, and E has been lowered to E♭.

The notes F and E♭ are enclosed to highlight the fact that they do not belong to the G major scale.

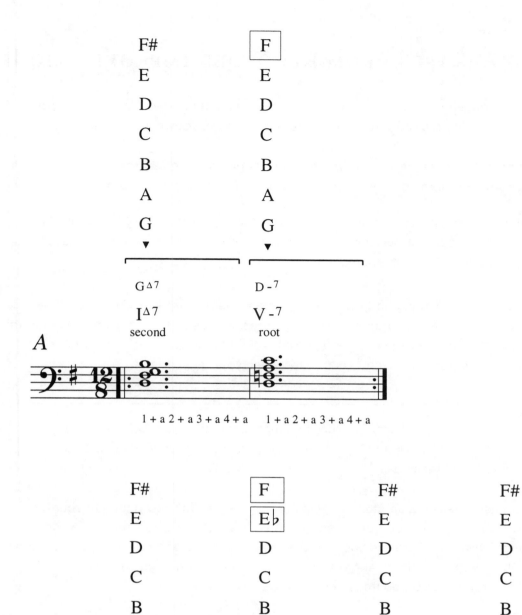

A

$G\triangle 7$ $D-7$

$I\triangle 7$ $V-7$

second   root

1 + a 2 + a 3 + a 4 + a   1 + a 2 + a 3 + a 4 + a

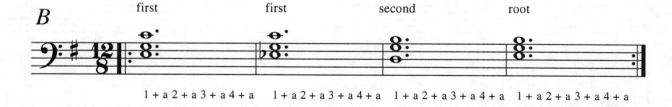

B

C   C-   G   E-

IV   IV-   I   VI-

first   first   second   root

1 + a 2 + a 3 + a 4 + a   1 + a 2 + a 3 + a 4 + a   1 + a 2 + a 3 + a 4 + a   1 + a 2 + a 3 + a 4 + a

When you improvise over this accompaniment, stay in each section for as long as you like. Also, go back and forth between sections as many times as you like. End your improvisation on the I△7 chord if you end in Section A; end on the **I** triad if you end in Section B.

INCORPORATING PHRASES FROM RECORDED IMPROVISATIONS

This Workshop—introduced in Book One—shows you how to learn phrases from the recorded improvisations, and encourages you to include these phrases in your own improvisations.

- Learning the phrases will strengthen your ear, provide insight into the recorded improvisations, and help prepare you for learning directly from the music of your favorite artists.

- Incorporating the phrases into your improvisations will challenge and sharpen your musical memory, add variety to your improvisations, and perhaps spark your imagination in ways that lead your improvisations in new directions.

Piano by Ear's approach to learning and transcribing phrases is presented in five steps. The guidelines enclosed in a box apply to the transcribing process in general. The guidelines that are *not* in a box apply to the first phrase of Track 9, which is the phrase you'll be transcribing in a moment. Listen to the recording through headphones when you transcribe.

Step 1

> Choose a phrase that you like from the recorded improvisation. If your CD player has a *minute/second* display, jot down the time displayed at the start of your phrase. This will enable you to find the phrase easily.
>
> To learn the phrase, press *pause* after the first note. With this note resonating in your ear, find it on your keyboard; then jot it down on the upper staff. (As you can see below, an upper staff and a lower staff are provided for the transcription.) Don't concern yourself with the rhythm right now. For clarity, make your notes small, centering them carefully on the appropriate line or in the appropriate space.
>
> Repeat Step 1 for each note in the phrase. *You may discover that you can figure out more than one note at a time—if so, you won't need to stop the recording after each note.*

Using the above guidelines, figure out the notes of Track 9's first phrase and jot them down on the upper staff; the first two notes of the phrase have been transcribed for you. (Remember that F♯ is in the key signature.)

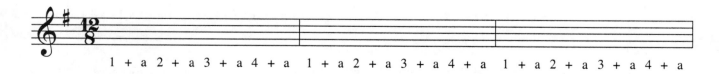

Check your work on the next page.

The notes in Track 9's first phrase are:

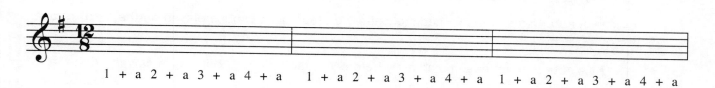

1 + a 2 + a 3 + a 4 + a   1 + a 2 + a 3 + a 4 + a   1 + a 2 + a 3 + a 4 + a

Step 2

Listen to the improvisation and tap the beats of each measure with your left hand:

- tap beat 1 with your thumb

- beat 2 with your 2nd (index) finger

- beat 3 with your 3rd (middle) finger

- and beat 4 with your 4th (ring) finger

It's *very helpful* to watch your fingers as you tap so that you can, in effect, see the beats as well as hear them. It's also helpful to tap on your thigh so that you can feel the beats in your body.

Two measures of percussion are played before the improvisation begins. Start tapping in the second measure as shown below:

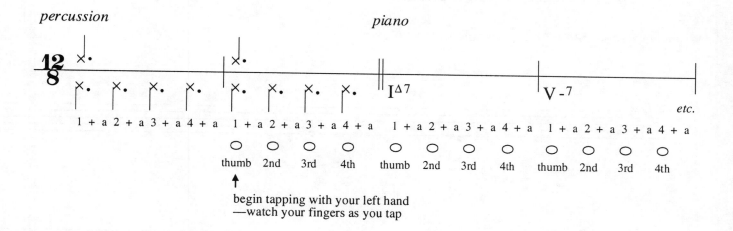

 Listen to Track 9, *watch your fingers,* and tap the beats as described above.

Step 3

Begin listening to the recording a few measures before the phrase you're learning. Tap the beats and watch your fingers as you did in Step 2. When the first note of the phrase is played, observe the position of your fingers:

- A note that sounds as you tap your thumb is played on beat 1.

- A note that sounds immediately after you tap your thumb is played on the "and" of beat 1.

- A note that sounds immediately before you tap your index finger, is played on the "a" of beat 1.

- A note that sounds as you tap your index finger is played on beat 2, and so on.

Once you've figured out the rhythmic placement of the first note, write it above the appropriate count in the first measure of the lower staff. Repeat Step 3 for each note of the phrase.

Rather than figure out the rhythmic placement of each note sequentially, you may find that it's easier to first figure out the notes that are played on a beat; then go back and figure out the notes that are played on an "and" or an "a."

Play Track 9, watch your fingers, tap the beats, and notice that the first note of the first phrase is played as you tap your middle finger. This tells you that the note falls on beat 3. Consequently, the note is placed above the "3" in the first measure of the lower staff (see staffs below).

Now return to Track 9, watch your fingers, tap the beats, and notice that the second note of the phrase is played just before you tap your ring finger, revealing that the note falls on the "a" of beat 3. Therefore, the note is placed above the "a" between beats 3 and 4.

Repeat Step 3 for each note of the phrase.

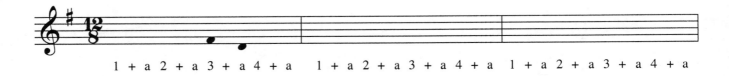

1 + a 2 + a 3 + a 4 + a   1 + a 2 + a 3 + a 4 + a   1 + a 2 + a 3 + a 4 + a

Check your work on the next page.

1 + a 2 + a 3 + a 4 + a   1 + a 2 + a 3 + a 4 + a 1 + a 2 + a 3 + a 4 + a

Step 4

> Listen to the recording and figure out which chord is being played when the phrase begins. Write this chord above the first measure. Once you've figured out the first chord, you can add the other chord(s) since you already know the order of the chords in the accompaniment.

 Listen to Track 9 and figure out which chord is being played when the phrase begins. Write the chord above the first measure. Now fill in the other chord by relying on your knowledge of the accompaniment. (The accompaniment is on page 38.)

1 + a 2 + a 3 + a 4 + a   1 + a 2 + a 3 + a 4 + a   1 + a 2 + a 3 + a 4 + a

Check your work on the next page.

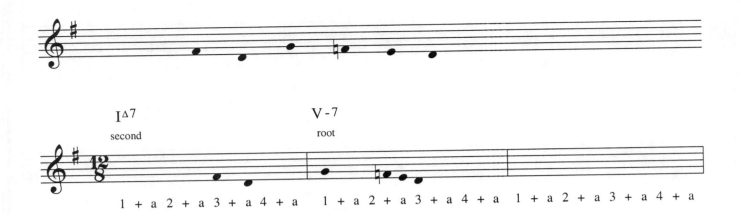

Learn to play the phrase fluently from memory, and incorporate it into your own improvisations. Fill out the accompaniment any way you like—you don't have to match what's on the recording.

Learn to play Track 9's first phrase (with the chords) fluently from memory, and incorporate it into your own improvisations.

INCORPORATING PHRASES THAT YOU'VE COMPOSED

As in Book One, you are encouraged to compose your own phrases and incorporate them into your improvisations.

- Composing is a great way to enhance your improvising skills—it gives you an opportunity to experiment with note combinations and rhythms without having to contend with the moment-to-moment demands of improvising.

- Incorporating your composed phrases into your improvisations will challenge and sharpen your musical memory, anchor your improvisations with music that is *tried and true,* and serve as a springboard for the phrases you create while improvising.

You can use essentially the same transcribing method you used to transcribe from the CD:

- Write down the notes of the phrase on the upper staff.
- Position the notes above the appropriate beats on the lower staff.
- Determine which chords accompany the phrase and write them above the appropriate beats.

WORKSHOP PROJECT

Compose a phrase or two on the staffs below. Write lightly in pencil and keep an eraser handy —you may want to modify a phrase after writing it down. Learn to play one phrase (with the chords) fluently from memory and include it in your improvisations.

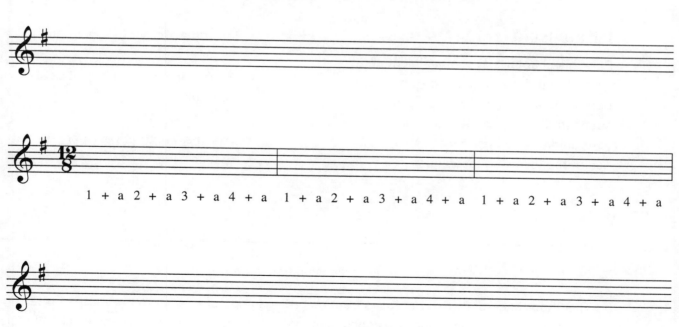

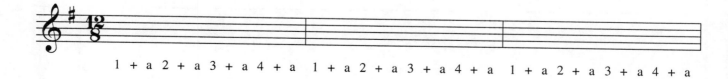

The Practicing Page

Playing *by heart* will strengthen your ear. For best results, learn to play the following activities from memory:

Chord Studies

Learn to play minor triads and minor-seven chords through the Cycle (pp. 35-36).

Review the chords introduced in previous chapters (p. 36).

Listening

Listen to the improvisations on Tracks 9 and 10 for ideas and inspiration, and to gain an intuitive feel for the music. Track 9 was created from the same set of guidelines you're using for your improvisations. Track 10 is based on, but not limited to, these guidelines.

Improvising

Play this chapter's accompaniment and count silently (p. 38). Join in with your right hand and improvise, using the suggested scales (p. 39). Let your ear be your guide as you improvise. Also, make use of the following techniques:

New! • Include the phrase from Track 9 that you've memorized (p.44) and the phrase of your own that you've memorized (p.45)

• Play with the two rhythms featured on page 32

• Include phrases that flow directly from one scale into the next

• Fill out the accompaniment

• Repeat melodic contours and rhythmic patterns

• Repeat phrases and parts of phrases

• Include eighth-note syncopation

• Begin phrases on different beats of the measure

• Vary the length of your phrases and spaces

Musicianship and Creativity

The importance of learning phrases from recordings and composing phrases, then weaving these phrases into your improvisations, cannot be overstated. The practice is invaluable for both enhancing musicianship and nurturing creativity.

Chapter Four

Diminished Triads & Half-Diminished Chords

[I'm] trying to get as much human warmth and feeling into my work as I can. I want to say more on my horn than I ever could in ordinary speech.

—Eric Dolphy
clarinetist / saxophonist

Chord Studies

Diminished Triads

The symbol for the diminished triad is " ° ."[1] To build this chord, begin with the minor triad; then lower the fifth a half step:

Build all twelve diminished triads and learn to play them fluently through the Cycle. Remember that the left hand begins the Cycle on middle C; the right hand begins an octave higher:

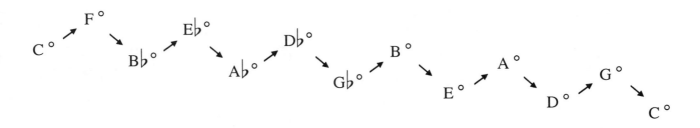

Half-Diminished Chords

The symbol for the half-diminished chord is " ø ."[2] To build this chord, begin with the minor-seven chord (-7), then lower the 5th a half step:

Build all twelve half-diminished chords and learn to play them fluently through the Cycle:

---

[1] Diminished triads are also identified as follows: dim
[2] Half-diminished chords are also identified as follows: -7♭5, min7♭5, m7♭5, MI7♭5

Chord Study Reminders:

- Say the letter name of each chord before you play it—listen closely to the sound of the chord.

- Be aware of the names of the chord tones you are playing: diminished triads (°) feature the *root, ♭3rd,* and *♭5th;* half-diminished chords (ø) feature the *root, ♭3rd, ♭5th* and *♭7th.*

- Practice your hands separately, then together.

- Choose a tempo that enables you to play in a relaxed and fluent manner.

- Learn to play the studies from memory.

REVIEW

Review the following chords by playing them through the Cycle. You may want to review just one type of chord in each practice session:

- minor-seven chords (-7)

- minor triads (-)

- dominant-seven chords (7)

- major-seven chords (Δ7)

- major triads

THE ACCOMPANIMENT

This chapter's accompaniment is in the key of B♭ major. Learn the accompaniment from Track 11 and transcribe it below. The transcribing guidelines are on page 37.

Notice below that in Section B, the first measure has two chords, and the second measure has three. All other measures in the accompaniment have one chord. Whether a chord is a triad or a seventh chord is indicated below the staffs.

The possible triads are:

- diminished triads (°)
- minor triads (-)
- major triads

The possible seventh chords are:

- half-diminished chords (ø)
- minor-seven chords (-7)
- dominant-seven chords (7)
- major-seven chords (Δ7)

Remember that B♭ and E♭
are in the key signature.

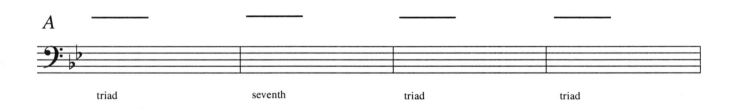

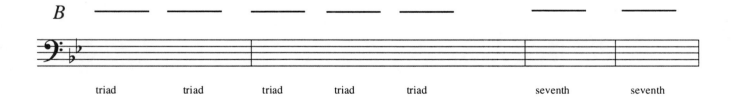

Check your work on the next page.

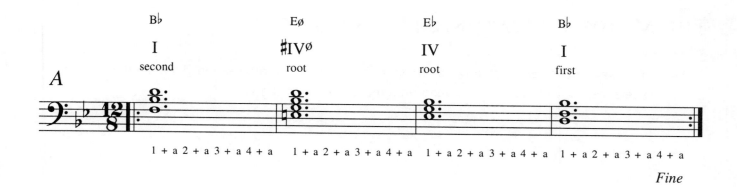

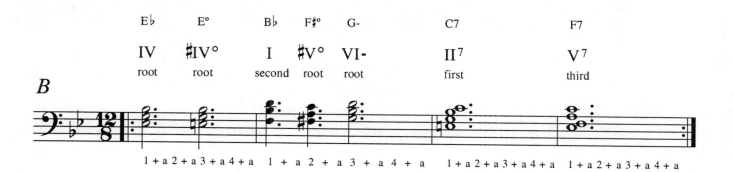

Learn to play the accompaniment fluently from memory. Chose a relaxed tempo and count to yourself in 12/8 time. Play the chords softly, and use the sustain pedal to create a smooth transition from one chord to the next.

When you improvise over the accompaniment, improvise within each section for as long as you like. Also, go back and forth between sections as many times as you like. End your improvisations at the *"Fine"* in the fourth measure of Section A. *Fine* (pronounced *fee*-nay) is Italian for *the end*.

THE MAJOR PENTATONIC (PLUS ♭3) SCALE

The *major pentatonic scale* will be used in this chapter's improvisation. To build this five-note scale, begin with the major scale; then remove the *4* and the *7*:

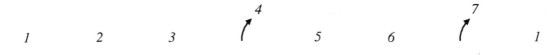

Now give the scale a bluesy inflection by adding the ♭3. We'll refer to this scale as the *major pentatonic (plus ♭3) scale.* The C scale looks like this:

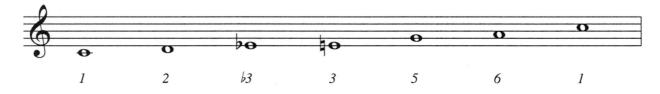

The B♭ major pentatonic *(plus ♭3)* scale will be used throughout this chapter's improvisation:

IMPROVISATION WORKSHOP:

EXPERIMENTING WITH ARTICULATION

When you improvise, you not only choose *what* notes to play and *when* to play them, you also choose *how* to play them. Within a single phrase, you might connect some notes smoothly to one another and play others in a short and detached manner. You might also accent some notes and play others very softly. *How* you play a note is referred to as *articulation.*

Articulation plays a key role in creating a mood and conveying emotion. Without it, music can sound stiff and uninspired—like someone talking in a monotone.

The art of articulation is learned through emulating other musicians, and through your own experimentation at the keyboard. Listen closely to the articulation used on the *Piano by Ear* recordings. Also listen to your favorite musicians—pianists, singers, horn players, guitarists, bass players—you can learn from all of them.

 Take a moment to listen to the improvisation recorded on Track 12. Pay special attention to the articulation.

TRANSCRIBING

The guidelines for transcribing phrases are on pages 40-45.

TRACK 12

Transcribe a phrase or two from Track 12 that you particularly like on the staffs below—remember to include the chord symbols. *Keep in mind that the notes of a chord that are played one-at-a-time belong to the filled-out accompaniment rather than the phrase you're transcribing.*

To check your work, turn to the transcription of Track 12 on page 56. Learn to play one phrase (with the chords) fluently from memory and include it in your own improvisations.

Drum Added

You may have noticed in the previous chapter that transcribing rhythms in 12/8 time is harder than in 4/4 or 3/4 time. To help with the transcribing process, a drum is played on each beat during the second half of the featured improvisations.

When you listen to Track 12, notice that the drum begins about halfway through the improvisation. Though you're free to transcribe any of Track 12's phrases, you may find it easier to transcribe phrases that are accompanied by the drum.

1 + a 2 + a 3 + a 4 + a   1 + a 2 + a 3 + a 4 + a   1 + a 2 + a 3 + a 4 + a

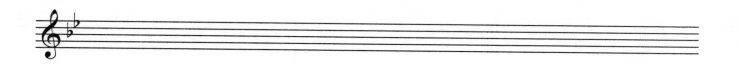

1 + a 2 + a 3 + a 4 + a   1 + a 2 + a 3 + a 4 + a   1 + a 2 + a 3 + a 4 + a

YOUR OWN PHRASES

Compose one or more phrases on the staffs below. Write lightly in pencil and keep an eraser handy—you may want to modify a phrase after writing it down. Learn to play one phrase fluently from memory and include it in your improvisations.

1 + a 2 + a 3 + a 4 + a   1 + a 2 + a 3 + a 4 + a   1 + a 2 + a 3 + a 4 + a

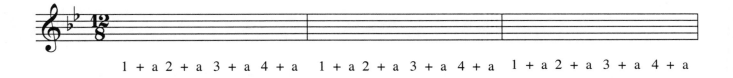

1 + a 2 + a 3 + a 4 + a   1 + a 2 + a 3 + a 4 + a   1 + a 2 + a 3 + a 4 + a

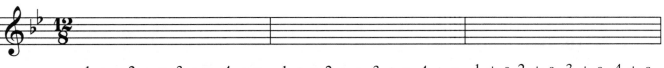

1 + a 2 + a 3 + a 4 + a   1 + a 2 + a 3 + a 4 + a   1 + a 2 + a 3 + a 4 + a

THE PRACTICING PAGE

CHORD STUDIES

Learn to play diminished triads and half-diminished chords through the Cycle (pp. 48-49).

Review the chords introduced in previous chapters (p. 49).

LISTENING

Listen to the improvisations on Tracks 12 and 13 for ideas and inspiration, and to gain an intuitive feel for the music. Track 12 was created from the same set of guidelines you're using for your improvisations. Track 13 is based on, but not limited to, these guidelines.

IMPROVISING

Play this chapter's accompaniment and count silently (p. 51). Join in with your right hand and improvise, using the suggested scale (p. 52). Let your ear be your guide as you improvise. Also, make use of the following techniques:

New! • Experiment with articulation (p. 52)

- Include the phrase from Track 12 that you've memorized (p. 53) and the phrase of your own that you've memorized (p. 54)

- Play with the two rhythms featured on page 32

- Fill out the accompaniment

- Repeat melodic contours and rhythmic patterns

- Repeat phrases and parts of phrases

- Include eighth-note syncopation

- Begin phrases on different beats of the measure

- Vary the length of your phrases and spaces

For best results, learn to play the above activities from memory.

TRANSCRIPTION OF TRACK 12

Find the phrase(s) that you've transcribed and check your work.

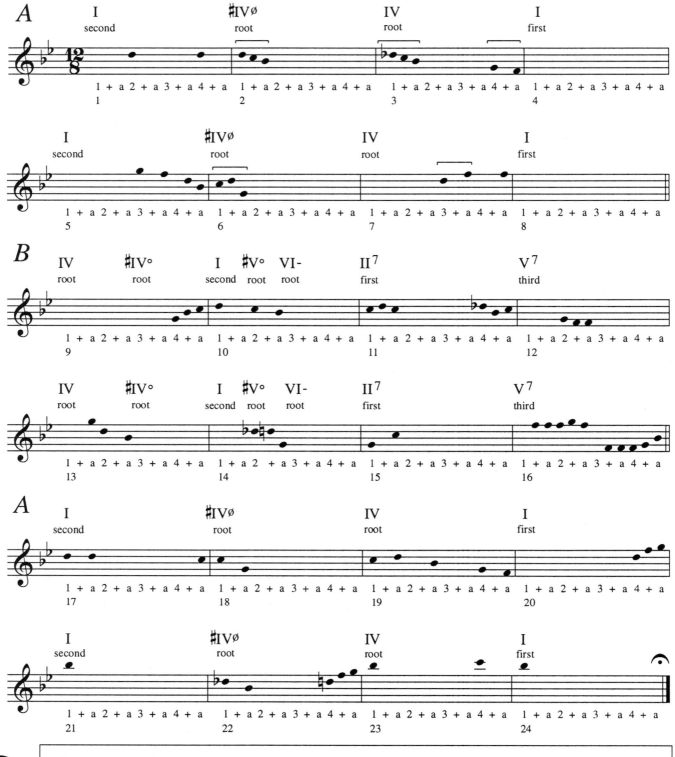

To benefit further from this transcription, listen to Track 12 and read along. Keep your eyes and ears peeled for examples of the featured improvising techniques. Notice, for example, the use of the rhythms introduced on page 32 (shown here without note stems or tied notes):

These rhythms are bracketed in measures 1 through 8.

Chapter Five

Diminished-Seven Chords

After you initiate the solo, one phrase determines what the next is going to be. From the first note that you hear, you are responding to what you've just played.... It's like language: you're talking, you're speaking, you're responding to yourself. When I play, it's like having a conversation with myself.

—Max Roach
drummer

CHORD STUDIES

DIMINISHED-SEVEN CHORDS

The symbol for the diminished-seven chord is " °7 ." [1] To build this chord, begin with the half-diminished chord (ø); then lower the ♭7th a half step. Lowering the ♭7th gives you a *double-flat 7th (♭♭7th)*. The ♭♭7th is the same note as the 6th on the piano, and for sake of simplicity, musicians usually write it and think of it as the 6th.

To build the C°7 chord, begin with the Cø chord; then lower B♭ a half step to B♭♭. B♭♭ is the same note as A on the piano and is written as A in the following illustration: [2]

Build all twelve diminished-seven chords and learn to play them fluently through the Cycle. Notice that C°7, E♭°7, G♭°7, and A°7 share the same four notes. Likewise, D♭°7, E°7, G°7 and B♭°7 share the same four notes, as do D°7, F°7, A♭°7, and B°7.

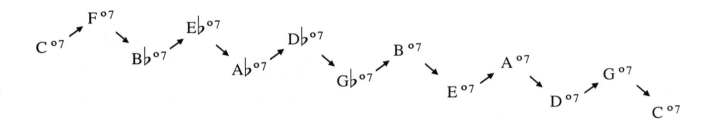

Reminders:

- Say the letter name of each chord before you play it—listen closely to the sound of the chord.

- Be aware of the names of the chord tones you are playing: diminished-seven chords (°7) feature the *root, ♭3rd, ♭5th* and *♭♭7th (a.k.a. the 6th)*.

- Practice your hands separately, then together.

- Choose a tempo that enables you to play in a relaxed and fluent manner.

- Learn to play the chord study from memory.

[1] Diminished-seven chords are also identified as follows: dim7
[2] If the ♭♭7th of the C°7 chord were written as a B♭♭, the chord would look like this:

REVIEW

Review the following seventh chords by playing them through the Cycle. You may want to review just one type of chord in each practice session:

- half-diminished chords (ø)
- minor-seven chords (-7)
- dominant-seven chords (7)
- major-seven chords (Δ7)

THE ACCOMPANIMENT
Guidelines: page 37

Learn this chapter's accompaniment from Track 14 and transcribe it below. It's in the key of C major, and may include any chord introduced so far:

- diminished-seven chords (°7)
- half-diminished chords (ø)
- minor-seven chords (-7)
- dominant-seven chords (7)
- major-seven chords (Δ7)

- diminished triads (°)
- minor triads (-)
- major triads

Check your work on the next page.

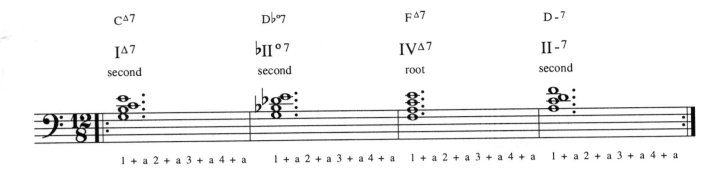

Learn to play the accompaniment fluently from memory. Chose a relaxed tempo and count to yourself in 12/8 time. Play the chords softly, and use the sustain pedal to create a smooth transition from one chord to the next.

NOTES FOR IMPROVISING

Each scale in the following illustration includes the notes in the underlying chord, plus notes that are complementary in the context of this improvisation.

The improvisation is in the key of C major, and as you can see, the C major scale is suggested for improvising over the I△7 (C△7) chord, the IV△7 (F△7) chord, and the II-7 (D-7) chord. The scale suggested for the ♭II°7 (D♭°7) chord contains eight notes rather than the usual seven. To build this scale, begin with the C major scale, then lower B to B♭, and add D♭.

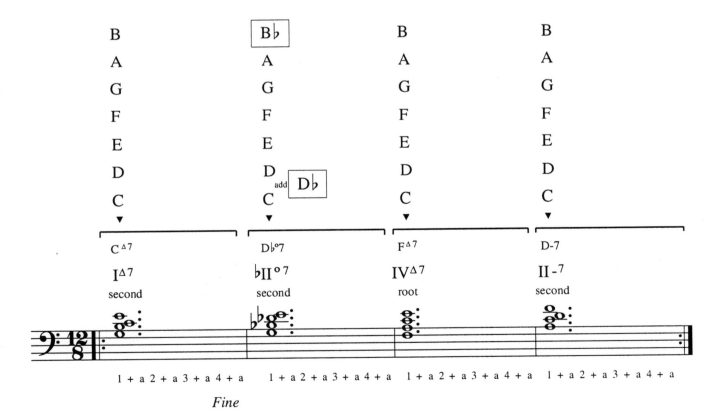

Fine

End your improvisations at the *Fine* in the first measure.

TRANSCRIBING

Guidelines: pages 40-45

TRACK 15

Transcribe one or more phrases from Track 15 that you particularly like. Check your work on page 64. Learn to play one phrase fluently from memory and incorporate it into your own improvisations. Remember that the notes in a chord that are played one-at-a-time belong to the filled-out accompaniment rather than the phrase you're transcribing.

Also remember that a drum is played on each beat during the second half of the improvisation. Though you're free to transcribe any phrase, you may find it easier to transcribe phrases that are accompanied by the drum.

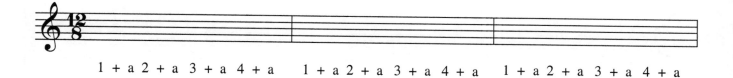

1 + a 2 + a 3 + a 4 + a   1 + a 2 + a 3 + a 4 + a   1 + a 2 + a 3 + a 4 + a

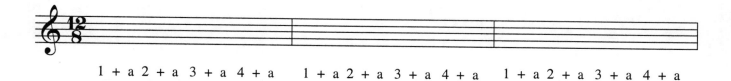

1 + a 2 + a 3 + a 4 + a   1 + a 2 + a 3 + a 4 + a   1 + a 2 + a 3 + a 4 + a

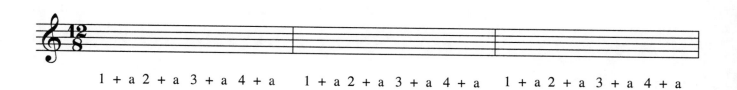

1 + a 2 + a 3 + a 4 + a   1 + a 2 + a 3 + a 4 + a   1 + a 2 + a 3 + a 4 + a

Your Own Phrases

Compose one or more phrases on the staffs below. Learn to play one phrase fluently from memory and include it in your improvisations.

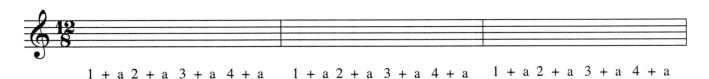

1 + a 2 + a 3 + a 4 + a   1 + a 2 + a 3 + a 4 + a   1 + a 2 + a 3 + a 4 + a

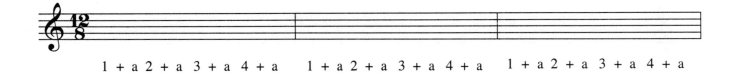

1 + a 2 + a 3 + a 4 + a   1 + a 2 + a 3 + a 4 + a   1 + a 2 + a 3 + a 4 + a

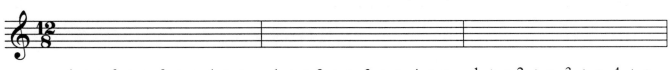

1 + a 2 + a 3 + a 4 + a   1 + a 2 + a 3 + a 4 + a   1 + a 2 + a 3 + a 4 + a

THE PRACTICING PAGE

CHORD STUDIES

Learn to play diminished-seven chords through the Cycle (p. 58).

Review the seventh chords introduced in previous chapters (p. 59).

LISTENING

Listen to the improvisations on Tracks 15 and 16 for ideas and inspiration, and to gain an intuitive feel for the music. Track 15 was created from the same set of guidelines you're using for your improvisations. Track 16 is based on, but not limited to, these guidelines.

IMPROVISING

Play this chapter's accompaniment and count silently (p. 60). Join in with your right hand and improvise, using the suggested scales (p. 60). Let your ear be your guide as you improvise. Also, make use of the following techniques:

- Include the phrase from Track 15 that you've memorized (p. 61) and the phrase of your own that you've memorized (p. 62)

- Experiment with articulation

- Play with the two rhythms featured on page 32

- Include phrases that flow directly from one scale into the next

- Fill out the accompaniment

- Repeat melodic contours and rhythmic patterns

- Repeat phrases and parts of phrases

- Include eighth-note syncopation

- Begin phrases on different beats of the measure

- Vary the length of your phrases and spaces

For best results, learn to play the above activities from memory.

TRANSCRIPTION OF TRACK 15

Find the phrase(s) that you've transcribed and check your work.

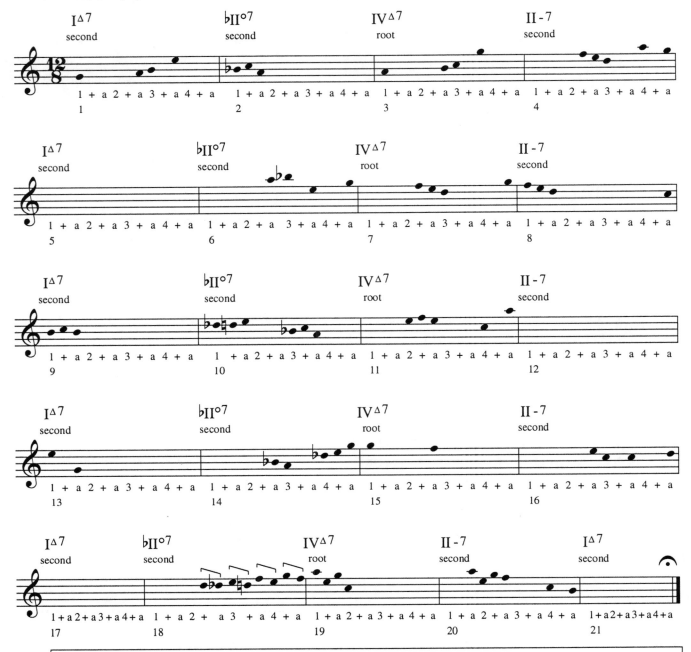

 To benefit further from this transcription, listen to Track 15 and read along. Keep your eyes and ears peeled for examples of the featured improvising techniques.

Also note the phrase in measure 18. It adheres to the scale recommended for the ♭IIo7 chord and follows a *down-one-scale-tone/up-two-scale-tones* pattern: after starting on D, the phrase moves *down one* scale tone to D♭, *up two* scale tones to E, *down one* scale tone to D, *up two* scale tones to F, and so on. We naturally hear this pattern in groups of two eighth notes. (See brackets over measure 18.) These groups of two eighth notes are superimposed upon the groups of three eighth notes that are an inherent part of 12/8 time. (Remember that 12/8 time subdivides the beat into three eighth notes.) Superimposing two-note groups over three-note groups creates a *cross rhythm*. Cross rhythms are used to great effect by jazz, rock, and blues musicians.

Chapter Six

Suspended-Seven Chords

I was quite intrigued by [Jerry Lee Lewis'] style—I'd never really
heard anything like it before. So I transcribed all his piano parts,
his solos—even the wrong notes! I became very adept at...writing
down music as I listened to it. This ability is very important and has
stood me in very good stead....

—Nicky Hopkins
pianist

CHORD STUDIES

SUSPENDED-SEVEN CHORDS

The symbol for the suspended-seven chord is " 7sus ." To build this chord, begin with the dominant-seven chord (7); then raise the 3rd a half step to the 4th:

Build all twelve suspended-seven chords and learn to play them fluently through the Cycle:

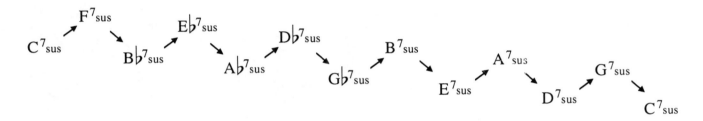

Reminders:

- Say the letter name of each chord before you play it—listen closely to the sound of the chord.

- Be aware of the names of the chord tones you are playing: suspended-seven chords (7sus) feature the *root, 4th, 5th* and *b7th.*

- Practice your hands separately, then together.

- Choose a tempo that enables you to play in a relaxed and fluent manner.

- Learn to play the chord study from memory.

REVIEW

Review the following seventh chords by playing them through the Cycle. You may want to review just one type of chord in each practice session:

- diminished-seven chords (°7)

- half-diminished chords (ø)

- minor-seven chords (-7)

- dominant-seven chords (7)

- major-seven chords (△7)

SIX CHORD FAMILIES

Chords that share certain basic characteristics belong to the same *chord family*. You've now learned one or more chords from each of the six chord families. The families, their defining characteristics, and the chords themselves appear below:[1]

Major Family CHORDS BASED ON THE MAJOR TRIAD THAT *DON'T* INCLUDE THE ♭7th

major triad ( )	root	3rd	5th	
major-seven chord (Δ7)	root	3rd	5th	7th

Dominant Family CHORDS THAT INCLUDE THE 3rd AND THE ♭7th

dominant-seven chord (7)	root	3rd	5th	♭7th

Minor Family CHORDS BASED ON THE MINOR TRIAD

minor triad (-)	root	♭3rd	5th	
minor-seven chord (-7)	root	♭3rd	5th	♭7th

Half-Diminished Family CHORDS BASED ON THE DIMINISHED TRIAD THAT INCLUDE THE ♭7th

half-diminished chord (ø)	root	♭3rd	♭5th	♭7th

Diminished Family CHORDS BASED ON THE DIMINISHED TRIAD THAT *DON'T* INCLUDE THE ♭7th

diminished triad (°)	root	♭3rd	♭5th	
diminished-seven chord (°7)	root	♭3rd	♭5th	♭♭7th (6th)

Suspended Family THE 4th REPLACES THE 3rd AS A BASIC NOTE OF THE CHORD

suspended-seven chord (7sus)	root	4th	5th	♭7th

---

[1] The defining characteristics used in this illustration don't tell the whole story but are nevertheless adequate for our purposes. Your knowledge of chord families will be put to use in Book Three.

THE ACCOMPANIMENT

Guidelines: page 37

 Learn this chapter's accompaniment from Track 17 and transcribe it below. It's in the key of F major, and may include any of the seventh chords introduced so far. The chords are listed here by chord family:

chord family:	major	dominant	minor	half-diminished	diminished	suspended
	Δ7	7	-7	ø	°7	7sus

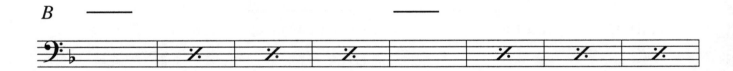

Check your work on the next page.

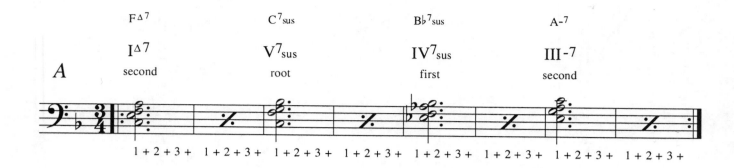

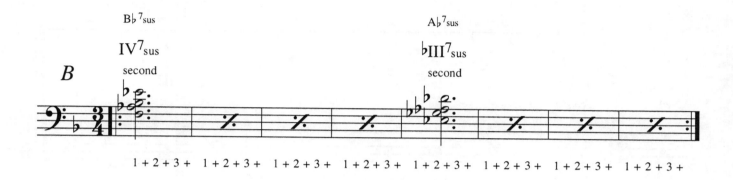

As you can see, this improvisation is in 3/4 time. Remember that in 3/4, the beat is subdivided into two eighth notes:

Learn to play the accompaniment fluently from memory. Chose a relaxed tempo and count to yourself in 3/4 time. Play the chords softly, and use the sustain pedal to create a smooth transition from one chord to the next.

NOTES FOR IMPROVISING

This improvisation is in the key of F major. As you can see on the next page, the F major scale is suggested for improvising over the I∆7 (F∆7) chord, the V7sus (C7sus) chord, and the III-7 (A-7) chord.

The scale suggested for the IV7sus (B♭7sus) chords has the same notes as the A♭ major scale. You can think of it either as the A♭ major scale or as a modified F major scale—one in which E has been lowered to E♭, D has been lowered to D♭, and A has been lowered to A♭.

The scale suggested for the ♭III7sus (A♭7sus) chord has the same seven notes as the D♭ major scale. This scale is relatively easy to use when you think of it as every black key plus the notes C and F.

Notes that do not belong to the F major scale are enclosed.

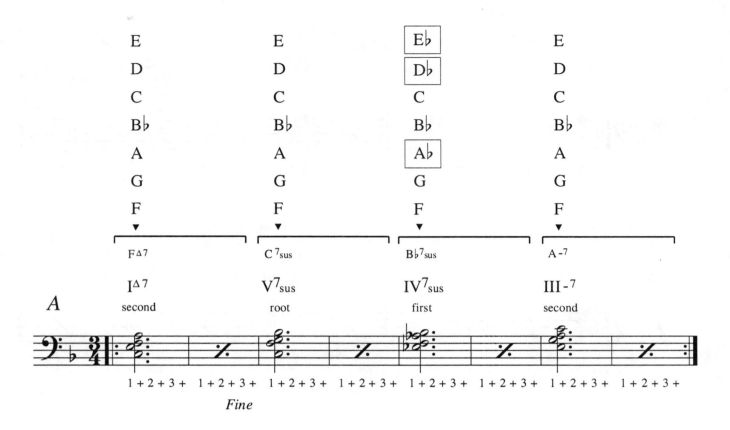

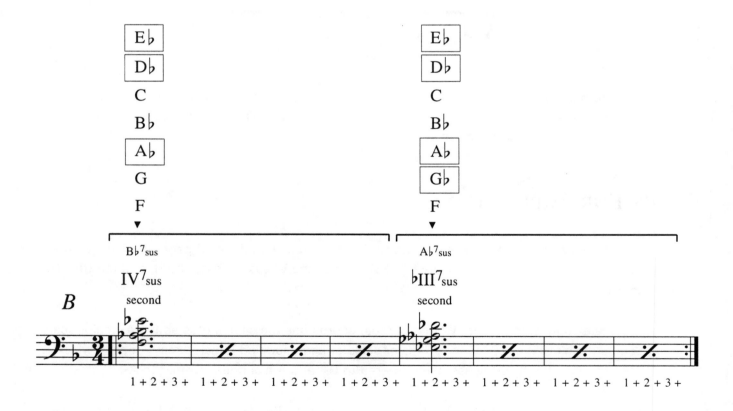

End your improvisations at the *Fine* in the second measure of Section A.

TRANSCRIBING

Guidelines: pages 40-45

TRACK 18

Transcribe one or more phrases from Track 18 that you particularly like. Check your work on pages 74-45. Learn to play one phrase fluently from memory and incorporate it into your own improvisations.

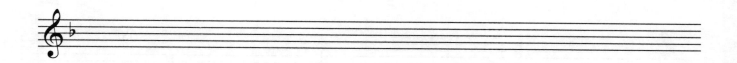

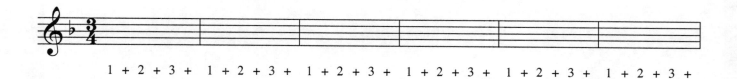

1 + 2 + 3 +   1 + 2 + 3 +   1 + 2 + 3 +   1 + 2 + 3 +   1 + 2 + 3 +   1 + 2 + 3 +

1 + 2 + 3 +   1 + 2 + 3 +   1 + 2 + 3 +   1 + 2 + 3 +   1 + 2 + 3 +   1 + 2 + 3 +

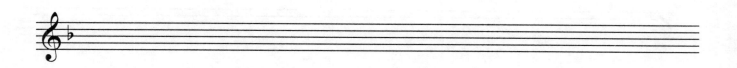

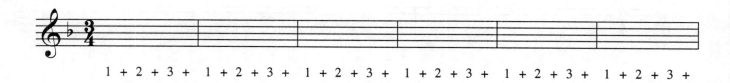

1 + 2 + 3 +   1 + 2 + 3 +   1 + 2 + 3 +   1 + 2 + 3 +   1 + 2 + 3 +   1 + 2 + 3 +

YOUR OWN PHRASES

Compose one or more phrases on the staffs below. Learn to play one phrase fluently from
memory and incorporate it into your improvisations.

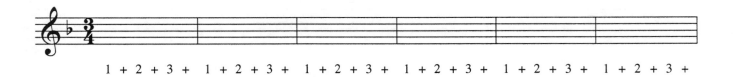

1 + 2 + 3 +   1 + 2 + 3 +   1 + 2 + 3 +   1 + 2 + 3 +   1 + 2 + 3 +   1 + 2 + 3 +

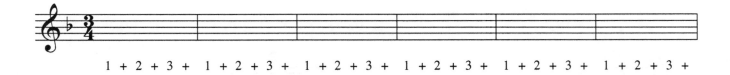

1 + 2 + 3 +   1 + 2 + 3 +   1 + 2 + 3 +   1 + 2 + 3 +   1 + 2 + 3 +   1 + 2 + 3 +

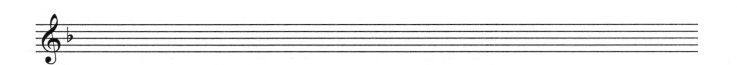

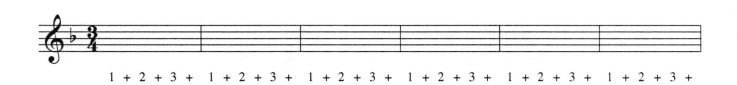

1 + 2 + 3 +   1 + 2 + 3 +   1 + 2 + 3 +   1 + 2 + 3 +   1 + 2 + 3 +   1 + 2 + 3 +

THE PRACTICING PAGE

CHORD STUDIES

Learn to play suspended-seven chords through the Cycle (p. 66).

Review the seventh chords introduced in previous chapters (p. 66).

LISTENING

Listen to the improvisations on Tracks 18 and 19 for ideas and inspiration, and to gain an intuitive feel for the music. Track 18 was created from the same set of guidelines you're using for your improvisations. Track 19 is based on, but not limited to, these guidelines.

IMPROVISING

Play this chapter's accompaniment and count silently (p. 69). Join in with your right hand and improvise, using the suggested scales (p. 70). Let your ear be your guide as you improvise. Also, make use of the following techniques:

- Include the phrase from Track 18 that you've memorized (p. 71) and the phrase of your own that you've memorized (p. 72)

- Experiment with articulation

- Play with the two rhythms featured on page 32

- Include phrases that flow directly from one scale into the next

- Fill out the accompaniment

- Repeat melodic contours and rhythmic patterns

- Repeat phrases and parts of phrases

- Include eighth-note syncopation

- Begin phrases on different beats of the measure

- Vary the length of your phrases and spaces

For best results, learn to play the above activities from memory.

TRANSCRIPTION OF TRACK 18

Find the phrase(s) that you've transcribed and check your work.

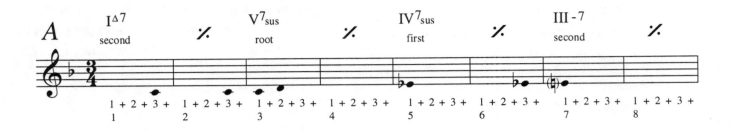

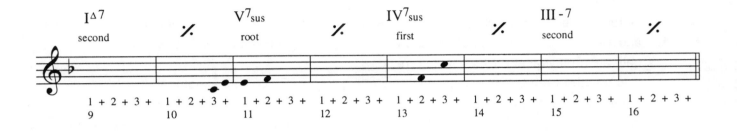

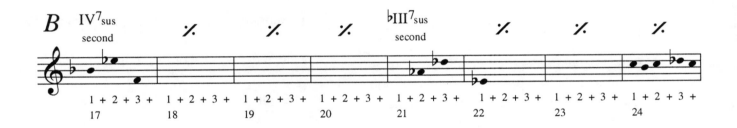

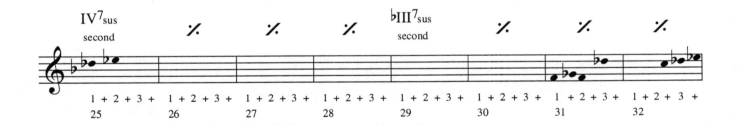

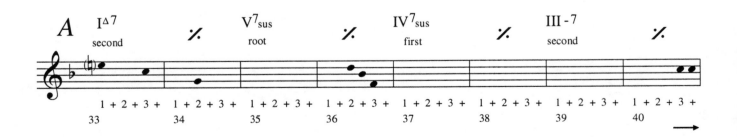

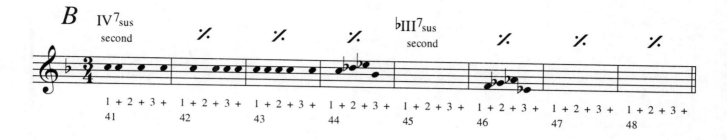

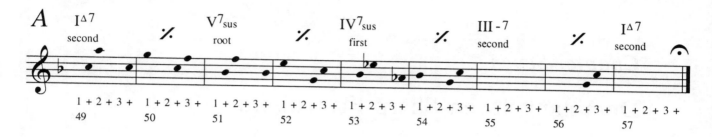

To benefit further from this transcription, listen to Track 18 and read along. Keep your eyes and ears peeled for examples of the featured improvising techniques.

Also notice that the right hand begins on C in measure 1 and gradually climbs to F in measure 11. When you listen to the recording, notice how this gradual ascent creates continuity—the phrases in these eleven measures sound as though they're united in the common goal of reaching increasingly higher notes on the keyboard.

Chapter Seven

Dominant-Seven-Sharp-Five Chords

John [Coltrane] even practiced between sets in the back room. He worked hard, like a person who didn't have any talent. As great as he was, he practiced constantly. So who am I not to?

—McCoy Tyner
pianist

CHORD STUDIES

DOMINANT-SEVEN-SHARP-FIVE CHORDS

The symbol for the dominant-seven-sharp-five chord is " 7+5 ." [1] To build this dominant family chord, begin with the dominant-seven chord (7); then raise the 5th a half step:

Build all twelve dominant-seven-sharp-five chords and learn to play them fluently through the Cycle:

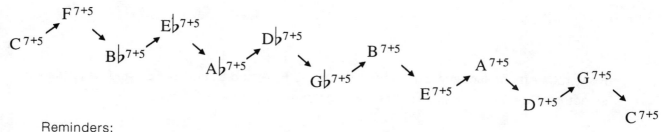

Reminders:

- Say the letter name of each chord before you play it—listen closely to the sound of the chord.

- Be aware of the names of the chord tones you are playing: dominant-seven-sharp-five chords (7+5) feature the *root, 3rd, ♯5th* and *♭7th.*

- Practice your hands separately, then together.

- Choose a tempo that enables you to play in a relaxed and fluent manner.

- Learn to play the chord study from memory.

REVIEW

Review the following seventh chords by playing them through the Cycle. You may want to review just one type of chord in each practice session:

- suspended-seven chords (7sus)

- diminished-seven chords (°7)

- half-diminished chords (ø)

- minor-seven chords (-7)

- dominant-seven chords (7)

- major-seven chords (Δ7)

---

[1] Dominant-seven-sharp-five chords are also identified as follows: 7♯5, +7, aug7

MAJOR TONALITY AND MINOR TONALITY

Major tonality refers to the underlying melodic and harmonic characteristics of music in a major key. As demonstrated throughout *Piano by Ear,* major tonality is based on the major scale. *Minor tonality* refers to the melodic and harmonic characteristics of music in a minor key—as you may have guessed, minor tonality is based on the minor scale.

Actually, there's more than one minor scale involved in minor tonality, but right now, we're only concerned with the *natural minor scale.* To build this scale, begin with the major scale, then lower *3* a half step to *♭3,* 6 a half step to *♭6,* and *7* a half step to *♭7.* The C natural minor scale serves as an example:

Now, rather than place flat signs in front of notes E, A, and B, add B♭, E♭, and A♭ to the key signature. Doing so will give you the key signature for the key of C minor:

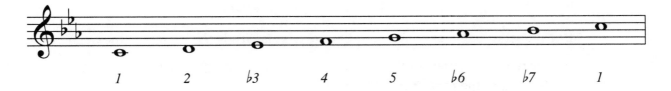

Notice that the key of C minor has the same key signature as the key of E♭ major, and that the C natural minor scale contains the same seven notes as the E♭ major scale. That's why C minor is called the *relative minor* of E♭ major, and conversely, E♭ major is called the *relative major* of C minor.[1]

---

[1] Each key signature is shared by a relative major and a relative minor key.

THE ACCOMPANIMENT

Guidelines: page 37

 Learn this chapter's accompaniment from Track 20 and transcribe it below. It's in the key of C minor, and may include any of the chords introduced so far. The chords are listed below by chord family—since the major triad has no symbol, it's simply identified as "major triad."

major	dominant	minor	half-diminished	diminished	suspended
major triad	7	-	ø	o	7sus
∆7	7+5	-7		°7	

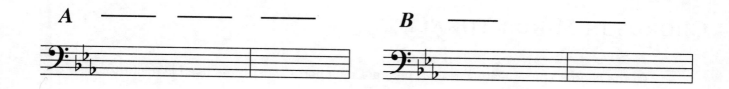

Remember that Bb, Eb, and Ab are in the key signature.

Check your work on the next page.

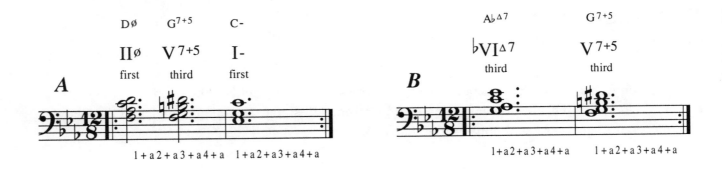

Learn to play the accompaniment fluently from memory. Choose a relaxed tempo and count to yourself in 12/8 time.

CHORDS IN MINOR TONALITY

Of the chords you've learned so far, here are the chords most often used in minor tonality:

I-	IIø	♭III△7	IV-	V7	♭VI△7	VIø	♭VII7	VII°
	II7		IV-7	V7+5	♭VI7			VII°7

NOTES FOR IMPROVISING

The C natural minor scale serves as the basic scale in this improvisation. The notes A and B are enclosed to highlight the fact that they do not belong to the scale:

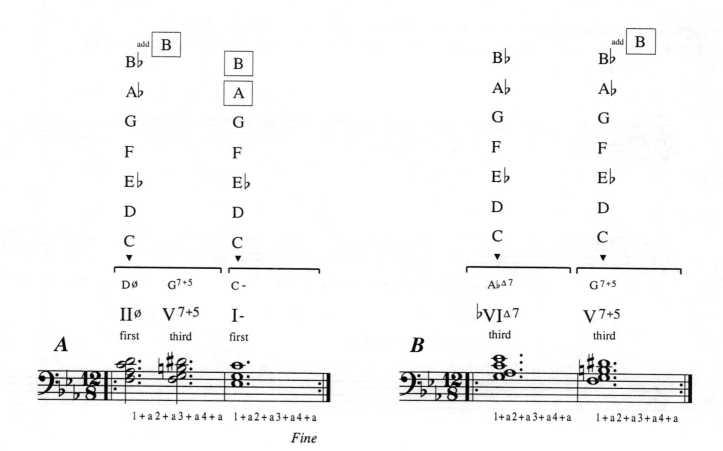

End your improvisations at the *Fine* in Section A.

TRANSCRIBING

Guidelines: pages 40-45

TRACK 21

Transcribe one or more phrases from Track 21 that you particularly like. Check your work on page 85. Learn to play one phrase fluently from memory and incorporate it into your own improvisations.

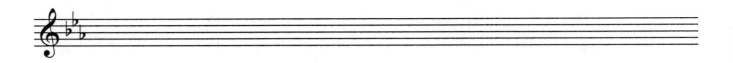

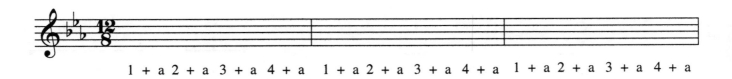

1 + a 2 + a 3 + a 4 + a 1 + a 2 + a 3 + a 4 + a 1 + a 2 + a 3 + a 4 + a

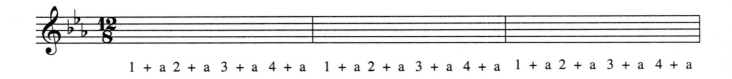

1 + a 2 + a 3 + a 4 + a 1 + a 2 + a 3 + a 4 + a 1 + a 2 + a 3 + a 4 + a

1 + a 2 + a 3 + a 4 + a 1 + a 2 + a 3 + a 4 + a 1 + a 2 + a 3 + a 4 + a

YOUR OWN PHRASES

Compose one or more phrases on the staffs below. Learn to play one phrase fluently from memory and incorporate it into your improvisations.

1 + a 2 + a 3 + a 4 + a   1 + a 2 + a 3 + a 4 + a   1 + a 2 + a 3 + a 4 + a

1 + a 2 + a 3 + a 4 + a   1 + a 2 + a 3 + a 4 + a   1 + a 2 + a 3 + a 4 + a

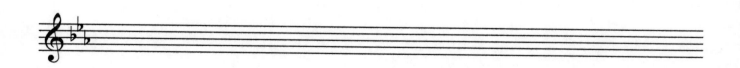

1 + a 2 + a 3 + a 4 + a   1 + a 2 + a 3 + a 4 + a   1 + a 2 + a 3 + a 4 + a

CHORD STUDIES

Learn to play dominant-seven-sharp-five chords through the Cycle (p. 77).

Review the seventh chords introduced in previous chapters (p. 77).

LISTENING

Listen to the improvisations on Tracks 21 and 22 for ideas and inspiration, and to gain an intuitive feel for the music. Track 21 was created from the same set of guidelines you're using for your improvisations. Track 22 is based on, but not limited to, these guidelines.

IMPROVISING

Play this chapter's accompaniment and count silently (p. 80). Join in with your right hand and improvise, using the suggested scales (p. 81). Let your ear be your guide as you improvise. Also, make use of the following techniques:

- Include the phrase from Track 21 that you've memorized (p. 82) and the phrase of your own that you've memorized (p. 83).

- Experiment with articulation

- Play with the two rhythms featured on page 32

- Include phrases that flow directly from one scale into the next

- Fill out the accompaniment

- Repeat melodic contours and rhythmic patterns

- Repeat phrases and parts of phrases

- Include eighth-note syncopation

- Begin phrases on different beats of the measure

- Vary the length of your phrases and spaces

TRANSCRIPTION OF TRACK 21

Find the phrase(s) that you've transcribed and check your work.

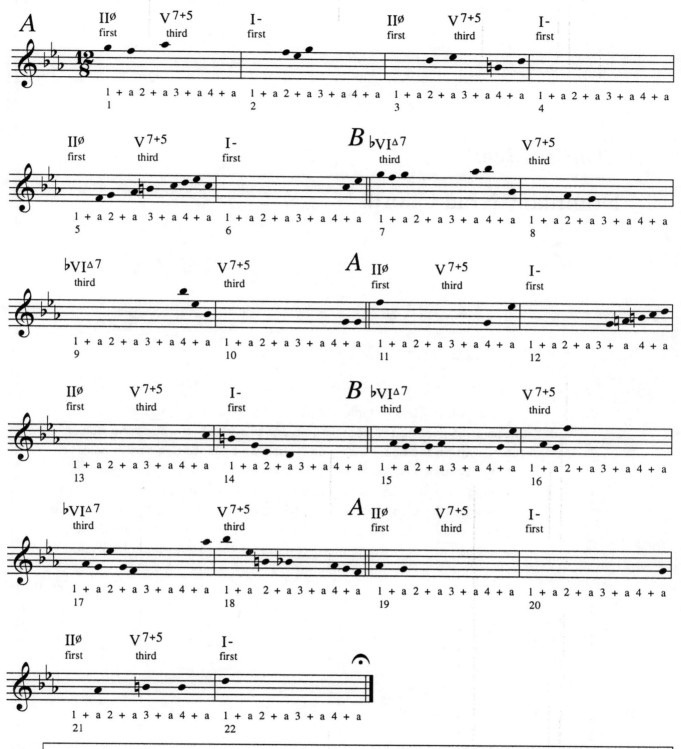

To benefit further from this transcription, listen to Track 21 and read along. Keep your eyes and ears peeled for examples of the featured improvising techniques. Notice, for example, that the first phrase (measure 1) and the second phrase (measure 2) have similar melodic contours* and *dissimilar* rhythms. When you listen, note that the similar contours create continuity, while the dissimilar rhythms contribute to the variety of the improvisation.

*melodic contour of the first and second phrases:

Chapter Eight

Dominant-Nine Chords

A slow blues curls out into the sunlight and pulls me indoors. Count Basie...is floating the beat with Jo Jones's brushes whispering behind him. Out on the floor, sitting on a chair which is leaning back against a table, Coleman Hawkins fills the room with big deep bursting sounds, conjugating the blues with rhapsodic sweep and fervor he so loves in the opera singers whose recordings he plays by the hour at home. The blues goes on and on as the players turn it round and round and inside out and back again, showing more of its faces than I ever thought existed.

—Nat Hentoff
writer

CHORD STUDIES

This chapter introduces chords that extend beyond the 7th. To build these chords, link two octaves of the major scale together. Number the notes of the first octave *1* through *7* (as usual) and the notes of the second octave *8* through *14*. The *1, 3, 5, 7, 9, 11,* and *13* of the scale become the root, 3rd, 5th, 7th, 9th, 11th, and 13th of the chord. The C major scale, and its corresponding chord, serve as an example:

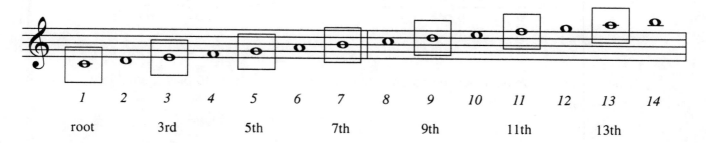

1	*2*	*3*	*4*	*5*	*6*	*7*	*8*	*9*	*10*	*11*	*12*	*13*	*14*
root		3rd		5th		7th		9th		11th		13th	

DOMINANT-NINE CHORDS (IN FIRST INVERSION)

The symbol for the dominant-nine chord is " 9 ."[1] This dominant family chord will appear either in first inversion or third inversion in *Piano by Ear*. To build the chord in first inversion, begin with the dominant-seven chord (7) in first inversion; then move the root up a whole step to the 9th:

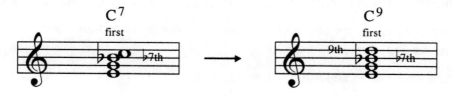

You may be surprised that this voicing excludes the root, yet *rootless voicings* are an important part of the jazz, rock, and blues chord vocabulary.[2] Build all twelve dominant-nine chords in first inversion, and learn to play them fluently through the Cycle:

C⁹ → F⁹ → B♭⁹ → E♭⁹ → A♭⁹ → D♭⁹ → G♭⁹ → B⁹ → E⁹ → A⁹ → D⁹ → G⁹ → C⁹

---

[1] Dominant-nine chords are also identified as follows: 7(9).

[2] *Piano by Ear's* voicing of a dominant-nine chord includes the same four notes as a half-diminished chord. C9, for example, has the same four notes as Eø. The distinction between these chords comes to light when considered in a musical context.

DOMINANT-NINE CHORDS (IN THIRD INVERSION)

To build the dominant-nine chord in third inversion, begin with the dominant-seven chord (7) in third inversion; then raise the root a whole step to the 9th:

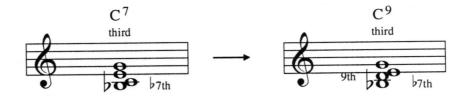

Build all twelve dominant-nine chords in third inversion, and learn to play them fluently through the Cycle:

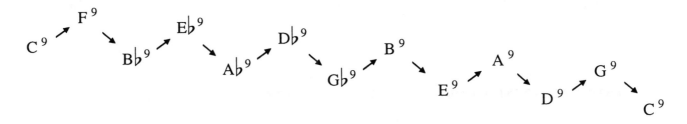

Chord Study Reminders:

- Say the letter name of each chord before you play it—listen closely to the sound of the chord.
- Be aware of the names of the chord tones you are playing: these dominant-nine chords (9) feature the *3rd, 5th, b7th,* and *9th.*
- Practice your hands separately, then together.
- Choose a tempo that enables you to play in a relaxed and fluent manner.
- Learn to play the studies from memory.

REVIEW

Review the following chords by playing them through the Cycle. You may want to review just one type of chord in each practice session:

- dominant-seven-sharp-five chords (7+5)
- suspended-seven chords (7sus)
- diminished-seven chords (°7)
- half-diminished chords (ø)
- minor-seven chords (-7)
- dominant-seven chords (7)
- major-seven chords (Δ7)

THE ACCOMPANIMENT

Guidelines: page 37

 This chapter's improvisation is a *twelve-bar blues,* which means that it's a blues based on a twelve-bar accompaniment.[1] Learn the accompaniment from Track 23 and transcribe it below. The accompaniment is in the key of B♭ and may include any of the following chords:

major	dominant	minor	half-diminished	diminished	suspended
Δ7	7	-7	ø	°7	7sus
	7+5				
	9 [first & third inversion only]				

Check your work on the next page.

---

[1] Though twelve-bar accompaniments are the most common, eight-bar, sixteen-bar, and twenty-four-bar accompaniments are also well-established forms. Blues accompaniments will be discussed in greater detail in Book Three.

Learn to play the accompaniment fluently from memory. Chose a relaxed tempo and count to yourself in 12/8 time.

When you improvise over this accompaniment, end at the *Fine* in the first measure.

NOTES FOR IMPROVISING

The blues scale was introduced in Chapter Two and is featured again here. Since this chapter's improvisation is in the key of Bb, you'll be using the notes of the Bb blues scale to improvise:

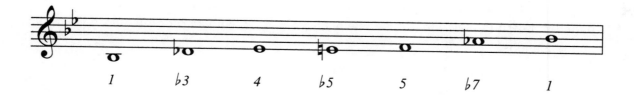

GRACE NOTES

A note played for a split second as an embellishment in front of another note is called a *grace note*. Grace notes—notated as little eighth notes with slashes through their flags—are used to great effect by jazz, rock, and blues musicians. When you improvise, experiment with using Eb as a grace note in front of E, and E as a grace note in front of F. Use two adjacent fingers to play the grace note and the principal note:

 The first two measures of the improvisation recorded on Track 24 are transcribed below. Notice the grace note at the end of the second measure—listen to the recording.

TRANSCRIBING

Guidelines: pages 40-45

TRACK 24

Transcribe one or more phrases from Track 24 that you particularly like. Check your work on page 95. Learn to play one phrase fluently from memory and incorporate it into your own improvisations.

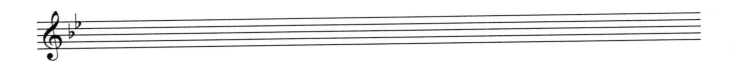

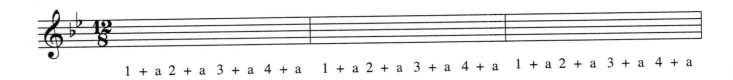

1 + a 2 + a 3 + a 4 + a   1 + a 2 + a 3 + a 4 + a   1 + a 2 + a 3 + a 4 + a

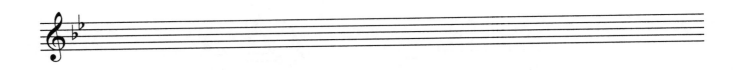

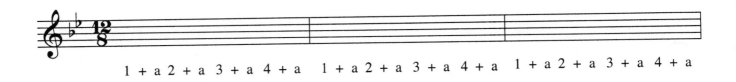

1 + a 2 + a 3 + a 4 + a   1 + a 2 + a 3 + a 4 + a   1 + a 2 + a 3 + a 4 + a

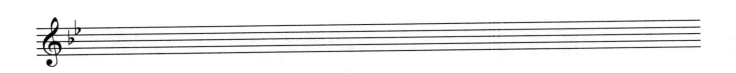

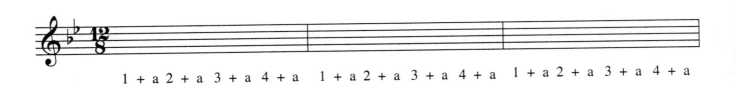

1 + a 2 + a 3 + a 4 + a   1 + a 2 + a 3 + a 4 + a   1 + a 2 + a 3 + a 4 + a

YOUR OWN PHRASES

Compose one or more phrases on the staffs below. Learn to play one phrase fluently from memory and incorporate it into your improvisations.

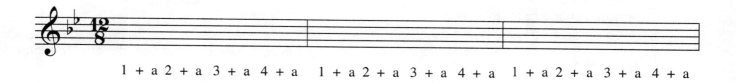

1 + a 2 + a 3 + a 4 + a   1 + a 2 + a 3 + a 4 + a   1 + a 2 + a 3 + a 4 + a

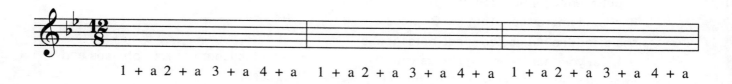

1 + a 2 + a 3 + a 4 + a   1 + a 2 + a 3 + a 4 + a   1 + a 2 + a 3 + a 4 + a

1 + a 2 + a 3 + a 4 + a   1 + a 2 + a 3 + a 4 + a   1 + a 2 + a 3 + a 4 + a

CHORD STUDIES

Learn to play dominant-nine chords in *first inversion* through the Cycle (p. 87).

Learn to play dominant-nine chords in *third inversion* through the Cycle (p. 88).

Review the seventh chords introduced in previous chapters (p. 88).

LISTENING

Listen to the improvisations on Tracks 24 and 25 for ideas and inspiration, and to gain an intuitive feel for the music. Track 24 was created from the same set of guidelines you're using for your improvisations. Track 25 is based on, but not limited to, these guidelines.

IMPROVISING

Play this chapter's accompaniment and count silently (p. 90). Join in with your right hand and improvise, using the B♭ blues scale and the suggested grace notes (page 91). Let your ear be your guide as you improvise. Also, make use of the following techniques:

- Include the phrase from Track 24 that you've memorized (p. 92) and the phrase of your own that you've memorized (p. 93).

- Experiment with articulation

- Play with the two rhythms featured on page 32

- Include phrases that flow directly from one scale into the next

- Fill out the accompaniment

- Repeat melodic contours and rhythmic patterns

- Repeat phrases and parts of phrases

- Include eighth-note syncopation

- Begin phrases on different beats of the measure

- Vary the length of your phrases and spaces

TRANSCRIPTION OF TRACK 24

Find the phrase(s) that you've transcribed and check your work.

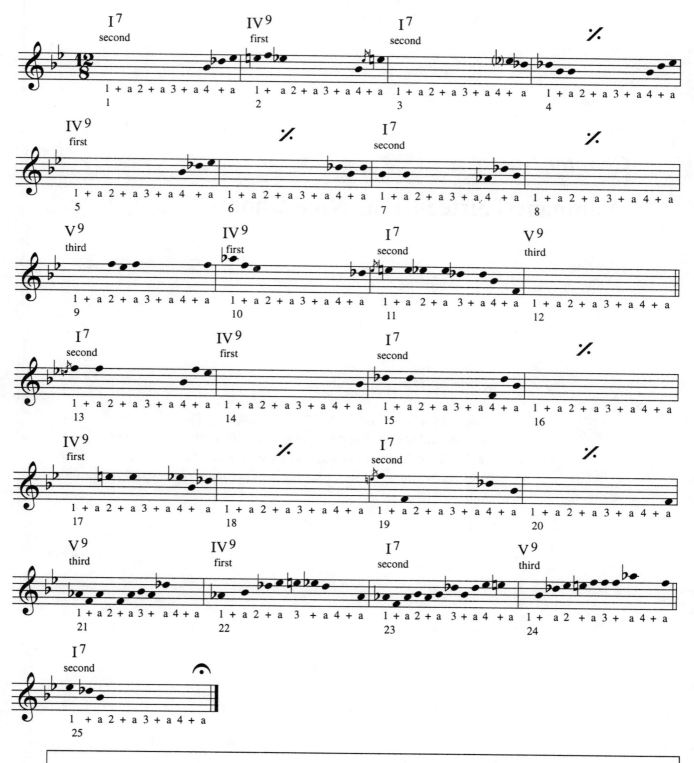

To benefit further from this transcription, listen to Track 24 and read along. Keep your eyes and ears peeled for examples of the featured improvising techniques. As suggested in Chapter Four, notice the frequent use of the rhythms introduced on page 32 (shown here without the note stems and the tied notes):

Chapter Nine

Dominant-Thirteen-Flat-Nine Chords

You have good nights and you have bad nights. But no night is ever just fantastic from the beginning to the end. Nothing is ever fully realized, and you never say, "Well, this is it." You're always on your way somewhere. To me, playing is generally a never-ending state of getting there.

—Art Farmer
trumpet player

CHORD STUDIES

DOMINANT-THIRTEEN-FLAT-NINE CHORDS

The symbol for the dominant-thirteen-flat-nine chord is " 13(♭9)." [1] *Piano by Ear's* voicing of this dominant-family chord includes the 3rd, ♭7th, ♭9th, and 13th:

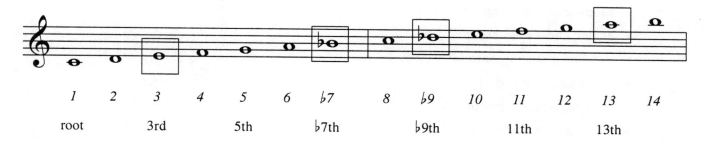

This rootless voicing will appear in third inversion only. To build the voicing, begin with the dominant-seven chord (7) in third inversion; then move the root up a half step to the ♭9th, and the 5th up a whole step to the 13th:

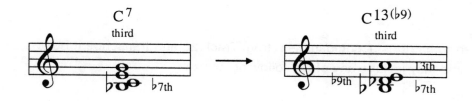

Build all twelve dominant-thirteen-flat-nine chords in third inversion, and learn to play them fluently through the Cycle:

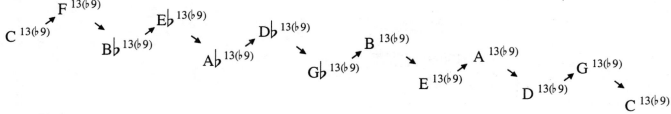

Reminders:

- Say the letter name of each chord before you play it—listen closely to the sound of the chord.

- Be aware of the names of the chord tones you are playing: these dominant-thirteen-flat-nine chords (13(♭9)) feature (from bottom to top) the *♭7th, ♭9th, 3rd,* and *13th.*

- Practice your hands separately, then together.

- Choose a tempo that enables you to play in a relaxed and fluent manner.

- Learn to play the chord study from memory.

---

[1] Dominant-thirteen-flat-nine chords are also identified as follows: 7 (♭9,13)

REVIEW

Review the following seventh chords by playing them through the Cycle. You may want to review just one type of chord in each practice session:

- dominant-nine chords [in first and third inversion] (9)
- dominant-seven-sharp-five chords (7+5)
- suspended-seven chords (7sus)
- diminished-seven chords (°7)
- half-diminished chords (ø)
- minor-seven chords (-7)
- dominant-seven chords (7)
- major-seven chords (∆7)

THE ACCOMPANIMENT

Guidelines: page 37

 Learn this chapter's accompaniment from Track 26 and transcribe it below. It's in the key of C major, and may include any of the following chords:

major	dominant	minor	half-diminished	diminished	suspended
∆7	7	-7	ø	°7	7sus
	7+5				
	9 [first & third inversion only]				
	13(♭9) [third inversion only]				

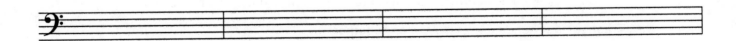

Check your work on the next page.

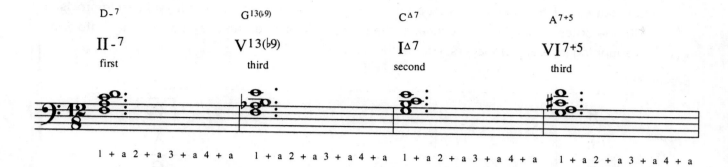

Learn to play the accompaniment fluently from memory.[1] Chose a relaxed tempo and count to yourself in 12/8 time.

NOTES FOR IMPROVISING

The improvisation is in the key of C major, and as you can see below, the C major scale is suggested for improvising over the **II-7** chord and the **I∆7** chord. The scales suggested for the **V**13(♭9) and **VI**7+5 chords include eight notes rather than the usual seven. The notes that do not belong to the C major scale are enclosed.

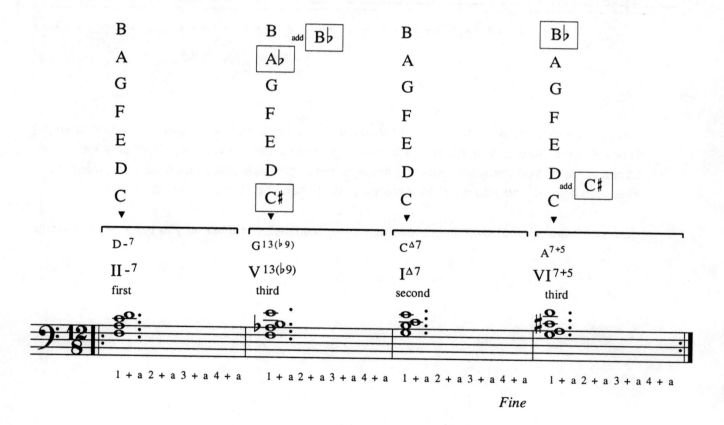

End your improvisations at the *Fine* in the third measure.

---

[1] The ♯5th the VI7+5 chord is actually an E♯—it's notated as an F to make the chord easier to read.

You can ease into this improvisation by dividing the featured scales into layers and improvising with the notes of one layer at a time. In the following example, the scales are divided into two overlapping layers. Both layers include the notes F and G:

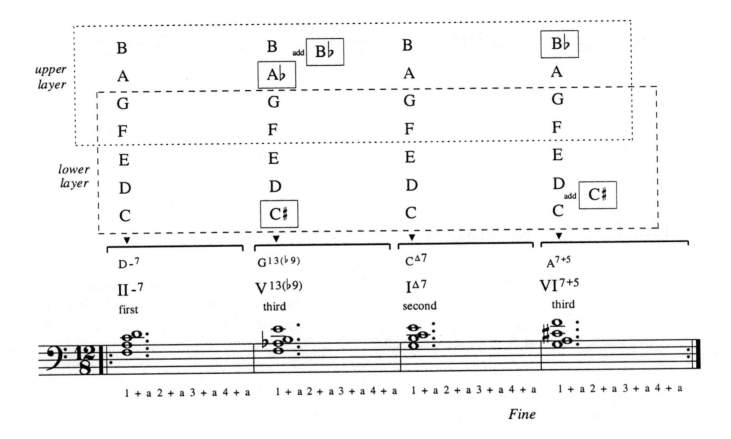

When you improvise with the notes of the lower layer, you'll be able to concentrate on changing C to C♯ in measure 2, and adding C♯ in measure 4—all other notes in this layer stay the same! Similarly, when you improvise with the notes of the upper layer, you'll be able to concentrate on changing A to A♭ and adding B♭ in measure 2, and changing B to B♭ in measure 4.

You can make up your own layers and include as many letter names as you think will be helpful.

TRANSCRIBING

Guidelines: pages 40-45

TRACK 27

Transcribe one or more phrases from Track 27 that you particularly like. Check your work on pages 104-105. Learn to play one phrase fluently from memory and incorporate it into your own improvisations.

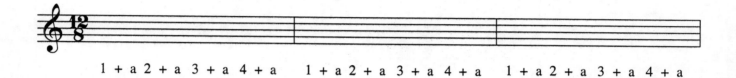

1 + a 2 + a 3 + a 4 + a   1 + a 2 + a 3 + a 4 + a   1 + a 2 + a 3 + a 4 + a

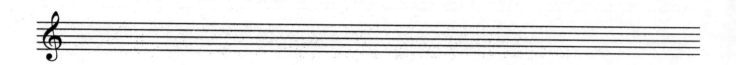

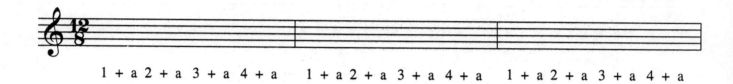

1 + a 2 + a 3 + a 4 + a   1 + a 2 + a 3 + a 4 + a   1 + a 2 + a 3 + a 4 + a

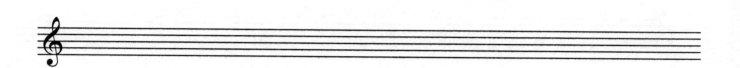

1 + a 2 + a 3 + a 4 + a   1 + a 2 + a 3 + a 4 + a   1 + a 2 + a 3 + a 4 + a

YOUR OWN PHRASES

Compose one or more phrases on the staffs below. Learn to play one phrase fluently from memory and incorporate it into your improvisations.

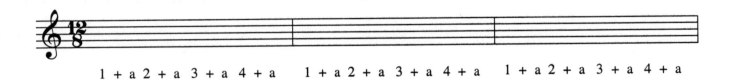

1 + a 2 + a 3 + a 4 + a   1 + a 2 + a 3 + a 4 + a   1 + a 2 + a 3 + a 4 + a

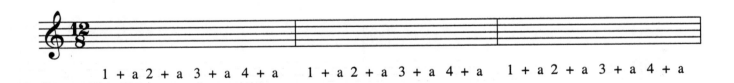

1 + a 2 + a 3 + a 4 + a   1 + a 2 + a 3 + a 4 + a   1 + a 2 + a 3 + a 4 + a

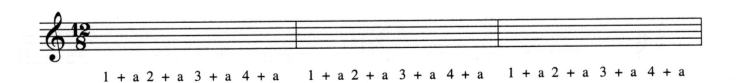

1 + a 2 + a 3 + a 4 + a   1 + a 2 + a 3 + a 4 + a   1 + a 2 + a 3 + a 4 + a

CHORD STUDIES

Learn to play dominant-thirteen-flat-nine chords in third inversion through the Cycle (p. 97).

Review chords that were introduced in previous chapters (p. 98).

LISTENING

Listen to the improvisations on Tracks 27 and 28 for ideas and inspiration, and to gain an intuitive feel for the music. Track 27 was created from the same set of guidelines you're using for your improvisation. Track 28 is based on, but not limited to, these guidelines.

IMPROVISING

Play this chapter's accompaniment and count silently (p. 99). Join in with your right hand and improvise, using the suggested scales (p. 99) and dividing the scales into layers (p. 100). Let your ear be your guide as you improvise. Also, make use of the following techniques:

- Include the phrase from Track 27 that you've memorized (p. 101) and the phrase of your own that you've memorized (p. 102)

- Experiment with articulation

- Play with the two rhythms featured on page 32

- Include phrases that flow directly from one scale into the next

- Fill out the accompaniment

- Repeat melodic contours and rhythmic patterns

- Repeat phrases and parts of phrases

- Include eighth-note syncopation

- Begin phrases on different beats of the measure

- Vary the length of your phrases and spaces

TRANSCRIPTION OF TRACK 27

Find the phrase(s) that you've transcribed and check your work.

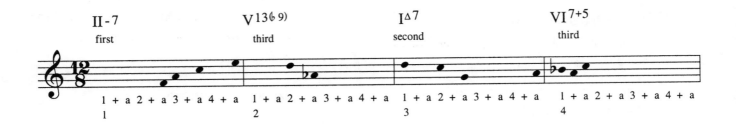

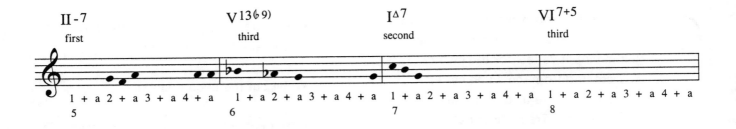

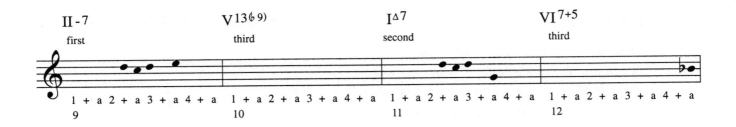

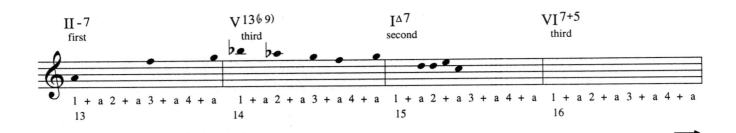

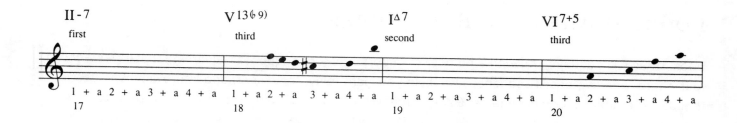

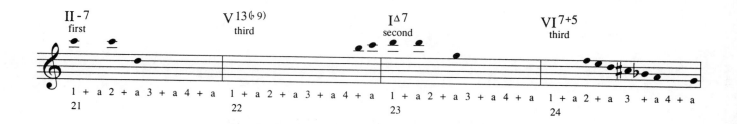

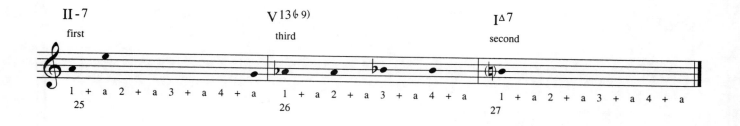

To benefit further from this transcription, listen to Track 27 and read along. Keep your eyes and ears peeled for examples of the featured improvising techniques.

Also notice that between measure 18 and 23, each subsequent phrase reaches a higher note. The first phrases (measure 18) reaches B; the second phrase (measures 20-21) reaches C; and the third phrase (measures 22 and 23) reaches D. When you listen to the recording, notice that this upward movement creates continuity—the phrases sound as though they're united in the common goal of reaching increasingly higher notes on the keyboard. (Also see remarks on page 75.)

LOOKING AHEAD TO BOOK THREE

Book Three will acquaint you with a number of important chord sequences—learning these three-chord, four-chord, and five-chord sequences will help you learn, play, remember, and improvise over literally thousands of song accompaniments. Book Three will also provide an introduction to scale theory as it applies to jazz, rock, and blues. Finally, Book Three will continue to serve as your guide as you develop your improvising skills through a combination of listening, transcribing, composing, and playing.

Congratulations on completing Book Two!

Appendix
SCALES FEATURED IN BOOK TWO'S IMPROVISATIONS

	Chords ▼		Scales ▼
Chapter One: C Major	I	C	C Ionian mode
	♭VII	B♭	B♭ Lydian mode
	♭VIΔ7	A♭Δ7	A♭ Lydian mode
	IΔ7	CΔ7	C Ionian mode
Chapter Two: F Major	all chords		F blues scale
Chapter Three: G Major	IΔ7	GΔ7	G Ionian mode
	V-7	D-7	D Dorian mode
	IV	C	C Lydian mode
	IV-	C-	C melodic minor scale
	I	G	G Ionian mode
	VI-	E-	E Aeolian mode
Chapter Four: B♭ Major	all chords		B♭ pentatonic *(plus ♭3)* scale
Chapter Five: C Major	IΔ7	CΔ7	C Ionian mode
	♭II°7	D♭°7	D♭ ♭II diminished scale
	II-7	D-7	D Dorian mode
	IV-	F-	F melodic minor scale
Chapter Six: F Major	IΔ7	FΔ7	F Ionian mode
	V7sus	C7sus	C Mixolydian mode
	IV7sus	B♭7sus	B♭ Dorian mode
	III-7	A-7	A Phrygian mode
	♭III7sus	A♭7sus	A♭ Mixolydian mode
Chapter Seven: C Major	IIø	Dø	D Phrygian mode *(add 6)*
	V7+5	G7+5	G Spanish Phrygian mode
	I-	C-	C melodic minor scale
	♭VIΔ7	A♭Δ7	A♭ Lydian mode
Chapter Eight: B♭ Major	all chords		B♭ blues scale
Chapter Nine: C Major	II-7	D-7	D Dorian mode
	V13(♭9)	G13(♭9)	G half/whole diminished scale
	IΔ7	CΔ7	C Ionian mode
	VI7+5	A7+5	A Spanish Phrygian mode

The author, three years old